GRIZZLY TALES

'CAUTIONARY TALES FOR

THE GNAUGHTY GNOMES OF 'NO!'

I hope you've brought a snorkel

IF YOU HAVEN'T, I SUGGEST YOU TAKE A DEEP BREATH.

CLOSE THE COVER BEFORE YOU'RE IN TOO DEEP.

Also in this series:
1. Nasty Little Beasts
2. Gruesome Grown-ups
3. The 'Me!' Monsters
4. Freaks of Nature
5. Terror-Time Toys
6. Blubbers and Sicksters
8. Superzeroes

GRIZZLY TALES

'CAUTIONARY TALES FOR LOVERS' OF SQUEAM'

THE GNAUGHTY GNOMES OF 'NO!'

JAMIE RIX

Illustrated by Steven Pattison

**THIS IS YOUR 5CM WARNING!
IN 5CM IT WILL BE TOO LATE TO SAVE YOU**

Orion
Children's Books

DO NOT OPEN THIS DOOR.

BEHIND IT THERE IS ONLY PAIN AND EVERLASTING TORMENT.

For Mum and Dad

First published in Great Britain in 2008
by Orion Children's Books
a division of the Orion Publishing Group Ltd
Orion House
5 Upper St Martin's Lane
London WC2H 9EA
An Hachette Livre company

Copyright © Jamie Rix 2008
Illustrations copyright © Steven Pattison 2008

1 3 5 7 9 10 8 6 4 2

The rights of Jamie Rix and Steven Pattison to be identified as the author and
illustrator of this work respectively have been asserted.

A catalogue record for this book is available from the British Library.

Printed in Great Britain

ISBN 978 1 84255 647 4

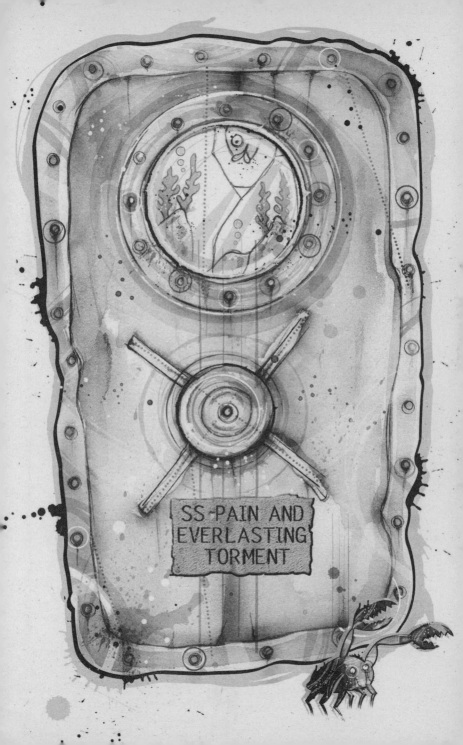

Now that you have been stupid enough to cross the porthole into hell and step aboard the SS PAIN AND EVERLASTING TORMENT you are doomed. Take a Life Jacket …

THE TAKE A LIFE JACKET

The Take a Life Jacket has been specially designed by Captain Night-night Porter to take your life and free up a cabin. If he tells you to abandon ship and put on a life jacket DON'T.

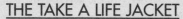

Padded Body Warmer – padded with lead. If you abandon ship wearing this you will sink straight to the bottom.

Hood – two positions. 1) Loose 2) Noose

Zip – concealed match head creates sparks against metal teeth and ignites nylon jacket. Go out with a bang!

Energy Sweets – good for shock (That is shock of discovering that the energy sweets are poisonous and will kill you before you can say, 'These energy sweets taste a bit poisonous.')

Whistle – to blow in the event of foul play (Unfortunately the pee is missing).
Light – by which to read your obituary in next day's newspaper.

Buckles, straps and ties – of no practical use, but will tangle around a propeller and ensure you are chopped up nice and small for fishes.

Flare – what you won't have anymore when you're dead.

BEWARE!
UNDER NO CIRCUMSTANCES PUT ON A TAKE A LIFE JACKET!

Welcome Aboard!

Today's Events

All passengers must check with the bursar that they have paid for their crimes in full or they will not be allowed to participate in the following events . . .

Quoits 12.00 hrs Top Deck. Throw horseshoes at small crying children. Removal of horses from shoes forbidden.

Ping Pong 15.00 hrs Officers' Mess. Shoot small pebbles from a catapult at live tethered boys and girls. *Ping* points awarded for the best sound on release of elastic. *Pong* points deducted if the boys and girls don't fill their trousers with fear.

Knobbled Knees Competition 17.00 hrs Tea Room. Guaranteed laughs as certified snitches get their knees knobbled. A must for all baseball fans.

Dinner N

The following guests are invited to di/e at the Captain's Table.

Gilbert Sparrow, Petula Ggambrel-Ffetlock, Josiah Reeks, Victoria Spew, Popering Partridge, Ida Lydon.

Weather Report

Not looking good for any of you.

Bon Damage!
Captain Night-night Porter

7

So glad you could make it . . .

The Hothell Darkness is a bit full up at the moment so I am using this floating prison ship. I mean, cruise liner called the SS Pain and Everlasting Torment to house all you lovely children until I can free up a bit more room at the hothell. Actually, the SS Pain and Everlasting Torment is not really floating. It's more sunk, as in lying on the ocean bed with a hole in its bottom (this makes it fit in with marine life, because everything that lies on the ocean bed has got a hole in its bottom, otherwise everything that lies on the ocean bed would eat and eat and then explode).

Come on in, the water's lonely!

Do stop crying! This wreck's taken on enough water already. You wouldn't be here if you hadn't been bad and if you've been bad you deserve it. *Of course* you've been bad. You're a child, aren't you? And all children are born evil. You don't believe me, do you? To prove that you are a child, answer this simple questionnaire.

1. Are you smaller than your parents?
2. Does your hair smell like a rugby sock?
3. Does dirt adhere to your skin like flies sticking to a windscreen on the motorway?
4. Do you wipe your mouth on the back of your sleeve

after kissing old people?

5. Do you eat the inside of your nose?

6. Is it more important to learn the shortcut to level 29 of *Resident Evil* than do your homework?

7. Do you float an air biscuit when you sit down or do any form of strenuous exercise?

8. When a dog cocks its leg in your direction do you put a bottle under the stream and keep it under the bed in case your big brother or sister gets ill and needs a glass of Lucozade?

9. Are you still hoping to win a Blue Peter badge?

10. Have you noticed that there are only nine questions?

15. Do you have difficulty counting?

If you have answered YES to all of the above there's a cabin with your name on it. If you have answered NO to any of the questions above you are a liar or are too old to be reading this book. Luckily, I also have cabins for liars and older book readers down here so you can stay. There is no ~~escape!~~ escaping the fact that I am a sensitive host who thinks of everything. (Sorry. Another slip of the pen. I can't get a proper grip with all this water.)

So why not sit back, take the weight of your ball and chain and let me ~~ruin~~ run your life. The SS *Pain and Everlasting Torment* is the height of ~~prison~~ cruising comfort. Thousands of ~~crustacean bait~~ satisfied customers have left testimonials in our Visitor's Book (or the *Book of Grizzly Tales*. as I prefer to call it). Why not read their stories and find out who you'll be sharing the rest of your life with. And after that your death. And after that your life after death. And after that your death after death. And after that . . . Actually there's nothing after 'death after death' except appearing on Big Brother. Anyway, you'll find you have so much in common with the other guests here. Pain and Regret being the main two things.

Take this poo away!
Do you think I've got a long face?
There do be dragons
        I'll scream till I'm sick!
GED BE AHT O ERE
Pump me up. I'm going down again

Those voices belong to the Gnaughty Gnomes of 'No!' What a bugnch of moagners! Gnever a 'yes' word betweegn them. They are all irritatigng childregn who say 'No' before they've evegn heard the questiogn. Do you — WAIT FOR IT! — kgnow what I meagn? Sougnds like you should be joigning them.

This first grizzly tale egnds up in so magny bits it's hard to kgnow where to start. So let's just plugnge in shall we, as Tinkerbell likes to say when the kgnives have been sharpegned.

CAPTAIGN GNIGHT-GNIGHT PORTER

TINKERBELL

We find ourselves in the town of Flushing Manners, on a street called Pernickety Road, behind a door bearing the name *Dunfussing*, at the table where Gilbert Sparrow sits down for every meal and stands up again two minutes later without having eaten a morsel. This is the same table at which sit his elderly, white-haired parents. Would it surprise you to know that they are both thirty-five, and that it is the stress of cooking for Gilbert that has turned their hair white?

> You should see the state of my hair after living on the SS Pain and Everlasting Torment for the last three weeks. It's an octopus.

Gilbert was a fussy eater. He never ate what his parents put on his plate, which meant they lived in a permanent state of worry that he wasn't taking in enough goodness and that one day soon his undernourished body would shrivel up and disappear altogether. But Gnomes of 'No!' gnever listen to common sense. No matter what his parents cooked he hurled it back in their faces with a cry of, 'Poo! Take this poo away!'

His parents watched television day and night, scouring the adverts for the latest faddy foods — cheese balls promoted by a famous footballer, alphabetti-spaghetti promoted by a famous children's writer or chicken nuggets promoted by a cartoon chicken with a limp.

You should try walking without nuggets. It makes your eyes water.

The next day, Mr and Mrs Sparrow would tear around the supermarket buying up stocks of these new foods, only to find that Gilbert refused to eat them, insisting instead on eating a sandwich, which was the only food that ever passed his lips.

'You won't try *anything*,' despaired his mother. Which was true. Since coming off the breast, Gilbert had resisted every new taste offered to him.

After the breadiness of rusks he went straight for sandwiches and one type of sandwich in particular – no salad or tomato or vegetables; no meat, ham or cheese … no goodness at all. Just jam.

***

Then, one day, Mrs Sparrow suddenly and quite unexpectedly reached the end of her tether. It was in the supermarket. She had been trying to interest Gilbert in a box of fairy cakes, advertised by Tinkerbell, the fairy from *Peter Pan*, when his screaming made her brain seize up. She rocked from foot to foot while singing a nursery rhyme over and over again. A small crowd gathered to stare at the wide-eyed woman and her eleven-year-old baby with a scrunched up face like a constipated ape.

'Nothing to see here,' cried the store manager, pushing through the shoppers. 'Move along, ladies and gentlemen. Are you all right, madam?'

'Is *she* all right!' screeched Gilbert indignantly. 'Is *she* all right? What about *me*? I'm the one who's being forced to eat poo cakes against my …'

Just then an unusual thing happened. The store manager took a pair of socks off the shelf and stuffed them into Gilbert's mouth so that his howling voice became a muffle.

13

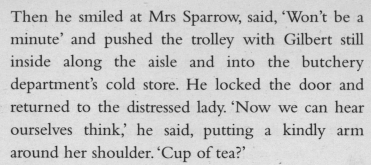

Then he smiled at Mrs Sparrow, said, 'Won't be a minute' and pushed the trolley with Gilbert still inside along the aisle and into the butchery department's cold store. He locked the door and returned to the distressed lady. 'Now we can hear ourselves think,' he said, putting a kindly arm around her shoulder. 'Cup of tea?'

It was the nicest cup of tea Mrs Gilbert had ever drunk, sitting there in the manager's office being told she was a marvellous mother while her son's cries were locked behind a six-inch steel door. The store manager was extremely helpful, and, far from pushing products from his own store as a cure (as you might expect) offered truly useful impartial advice. When Gilbert was released from the cold store he was still shouting, 'I only want a jam sandwich! You can't make me eat anything else.' But his mother was smiling and didn't seem bothered by the noise.

She held him firmly by the top of his arm and, nodding her head to acknowledge the applause of the other shoppers, dragged him home like a Christmas tree.

***

That night during a soup supper, she took a box of

fairy cakes out of her pocket and waved them under Gilbert's nose.

'The store manager made me fill it in,' she said excitedly, indicating an application form on the outside of the packaging. 'Your father and I agree that this might be the answer to your little problem.'

'My problem!' roared her son. 'You're the ones who keep cooking food I can't stand.' He threw his spoon into his bowl of minestrone.

'Do I look like I care?' said his mother, calmly wiping the flecks of carrot out of her eye. 'Do I look like I care, Mr Sparrow?'

'You don't,' said Gilbert's father.

'What's going on?' growled Gilbert suspiciously.

'Well,' said his mother, 'you're not going to like this, but in future, if you don't eat what is on your plate we will have to get Tinkerbell to come and *make* you!'

'Bravo,' said Mr Sparrow.

'You're pathetic!' snorted the boy. 'I can't believe that I am the product of two such feeble minds. Do you really expect me to be scared of a little fairy?'

'I think you should be,' warned his mother. 'Listen.' Then she read the out the blurb on the side of the fairy cake box.

'What have you done?' snarled Gilbert.

'Nothing,' laughed his mother. 'That nice supermarket manager did everything for me. He filled it in and sent it off. Apparently, Tinkerbell puts a magic spell on knives and forks so that when a child refuses to eat what's on their plate the cutlery cuts the food up and forces it down their gullets.'

Gilbert shook his head in disbelief. 'Tinkerbell is a *made-up* fairy,' he scoffed. 'She doesn't exist.'

'Oh it's not a *she*,' corrected Mrs Sparrow. 'It's a *he*. The store manager told me.'

'Have you lost your marbles?' shouted the cornered boy. 'Even little babies know about Tinkerbell – clap if you believe in magic – from *Peter Pan*. She's a *she*, and she's not real.'

Mrs Sparrow looked at Mr Sparrow and willed him out of his chair. He stood behind Gilbert and laid a heavy hand upon his shoulder 'It's time to grow up, son,' he said gravely, 'and face the real world. I mean there's lots of food I don't particularly like, but you don't catch me not finishing what's on my plate.'

'Me neither,' chipped in Mrs Sparrow. 'It would be impolite.'

'So for the sake of a more pleasant life all round,' said Mr Sparrow, 'let's have an end to this nonsense. What do you say?'

Gilbert stared at his feet for what seemed like an eternity. 'OK,' he said suddenly.

'OK?' gasped his parents with astonishment.

'OK, but here's the deal. If you eat everything on *your* plate for the next week I'll eat everything on *my* plate for ever—' his parents clutched each other's hands with excitement. This was everything they'd ever wished for '— on one condition,' said the boy.

'Oh,' said Mrs Sparrow. 'There's a condition?'

'Name it,' said her husband boldly.

'*I'm* cooking,' said Gilbert with a twinkle of sly in his eye.

We don't have a galley in The SS Pain and Everlasting Torment. We've got a gallows, but the atmosphere in there's not really conducive for cooking. Plus if you drop something by mistake it just falls through the floor.

They agreed to his plan. For one whole week Gilbert would cook for his parents and they would eat everything on their plates. One discarded piece of gristle or fish bone and the bet was off. What Mr and Mrs Sparrow had failed to agree before they accepted the wager, however, was the menu. Herein lay Gilbert's secret weapon. Over the next seven days, he cooked the most disgusting things he could think of so that his parents wouldn't be able to eat them: frog spawn milkshake; battered snake and stick insect chips; rancid ostrich eggs with black yolks that smelled like a marathon runner's feet; sweat glands from a frightened fox; skunk on a skewer; gelatinous gerbils; armpit hair pâté; bogey stew; terrapins on toast; toe jam pie and dung beetle pancakes with a sauce made from sweetened cat's pee. They ate them all. They knew what was at stake. They knew that if they choked on one mouthful or pushed their plates away they would lose and be right back where they'd started. So they held their breath and averted their gaze and thought about nice things while the beetles ran around on their tongues and the bogeys stuck to their teeth.

***

By the end of supper on the seventh day, Mr and Mrs Sparrow placed their knives and forks on the empty plates in front of them, wiped their lips on their napkins and pushed away their plates.

'Finished,' burped Gilbert's father. 'That was the best Ratburger I've ever eaten.'

I LOVE ratburger (with mousecapone cheese)!

'I especially liked the tail,' said his mother. 'I can still feel it tickling the back of my throat.'

The boy glowered at his infuriating parents.

'Well, there you are, Gilbert,' said Mr Sparrow. 'We've eaten everything on our plates for a week. So *we've* won and *you've* lost!'

'We've kept our side of the bargain,' said Mrs Sparrow, 'now it's your turn. What would you like for supper; sausage and mash or chicken pie with gravy?'

'NO!' The word exploded out of the boy's mouth

like a lead pellet. 'You haven't won. Not yet. The week's not up yet. There's still an hour to go, which means that I've still got sixty minutes to think of something you won't eat.'

'How about dust from the vacuum cleaner?' joked his mother.

'Oh no I rather like that!' laughed Mr Sparrow. 'Dust a l'orange – bring me seconds!

Gilbert hated being mocked even more than he hated losing. He stamped out of the kitchen with a promise to return within the hour, then ran upstairs to wrack his boiling brains.

Meanwhile, there was joy in the kitchen. Mr and Mrs Sparrow had cured their fussy son.

'There's nothing he can think of now that we won't eat,' Mr Sparrow chirped confidently. 'He can't win.' As he said these words there was a ring on the doorbell.

Now who THE DEVIL could that be?

Standing outside in the rain was a stinking tradesman. He was wearing a leather jerkin and a battered black hat which he removed to show his wrinkled face. He had long grey hair down to his waist, a chin covered in white stubble and jagged brown teeth like a broken fence.

'Any knives sharpening?' he said in a wheezing voice that squeaked like a metal wheel on a wheelbarrow.

'No thank you,' said Mrs Sparrow.

'You sure?' pressed the tinker, pushing his foot in the door as she tried to close it, 'only I got your form.'

Mrs Sparrow took her hand off the door and peered at the old man's yellow eyes. 'Are you who I think you are?' she asked hesitantly.

'That depends,' he said, 'on who you think I am.'

'Tinkerbell?'

'Sssh!' whispered the crinkled lips. 'Secret.' He pulled on a leather strap that was wound around his hand and a blue wooden drum on an old set of pram wheels rolled up to the front door. 'So nothing needs grinding then?'

Mr Sparrow appeared through the kitchen door. 'Mr Tinkerbell,' he said, 'delighted to meet you.'

'Not so much of the Mister. Just plain Tinkerbell

21

'… as in the fairy.'

'You're bigger than I thought.'

'I'm not *the* Tinkerbell,' rasped the old man, scratching his face with a blackened fingernail. 'I told that J.M. Barrie that if he wanted to use my name in that *Peter Pan* book he should paint me as I *really* is. But "no," he said, "children won't believe in a fairy unless she is pretty, little and buzzing with wings."'

'You knew J.M. Barrie?'

'Sharpened his knives every month. Stole my name, rotten thief. Still, what can you do? He's dead now and I'm still carving.'

'Look, I'm sorry if we've wasted your time,' said Mr Sparrow gently, 'but the fact is that since my wife sent you her wish on that form things have taken a turn for the better in this house, and although we might have needed your services then, we don't anymore.'

'Childrens never change,' said Tinkerbell, hoiking a plug of phlegm from the back of his throat and spitting it onto the front step. 'Never!'

'This one has,' said Mrs Sparrow.

The tinker sucked his teeth and laughed disdainfully. 'But what if he ain't?' he said. 'What if he ain't cured? And here's me on your doorstep offering a healing. Success guaranteed!' He pulled a pitiful face. 'This magic whetstone's my life. Sharpening knives and forks is all I know how to do. Won't you oblige an old man in his wishes, madam?'

'Oh dear,' weakened Mrs Sparrow. 'If it means so much to you ... I don't see what harm it can do.'

'None!' The tinker beamed. 'It's just harmless hexicography to make people eat what's on their plate that's all. And you get your cutlery sharpened into the bargain.'

'How much will it cost?' asked Mrs Sparrow. 'I don't imagine magic's cheap.'

'Madam,' said Tinkerbell haughtily. 'Do fairies mucky their hands with money or does they do what they do for the betterment of humanity?' He waited for an answer.

'The second one?' guessed Mrs Sparrow.

'The very same,' said Tinkerbell. 'I'll do it for free.'

***

It took less than ten minutes. Mr and Mrs Sparrow put their cutlery into Tinkerbell's drum and listened to it sharpening while the tinker turned the porcelain handle and sang to himself.

'Tinker, tailor, knife impaler
Whetstone, headstone
Morsel Me
Grinder, blinder, gut-rewinder
Sharp the blade
And eat for free

Dancing, prancing, lymph-gland lancing
Slivered lungs
And chopped-up knees
Plated, grated, ground and sated
Hand of doom
And foot of flees.'

No sooner had the tinker departed than Gilbert's parents laid the table for supper using the newly honed knives and forks. They were greatly excited, because this was the first supper that Gilbert would ever eat. Guaranteed!

Do you think I've got a long face?

Yes. Petty. you have. It looks like a ski jump.

When Gilbert thundered downstairs a few minutes later, however, he was smirking.

'I decided on chicken,' said his mother.

'Not for me,' sniggered the wilful boy.

'I thought we had a deal,' protested his father.

'We still do,' said the boy. 'Only there's still five minutes to go until the week is up.'

'I don't understand,' said his mother.

'So I've got one more thing I want you to eat,' said Gilbert, 'and if you refuse, I win.'

'We won't refuse,' said his father.

'Oh I think you might,' said his son, standing on a chair and lying across his mother and father's plates. 'Eat *me*!' His parents jumped up from the table.

'Are you mad?!' shrieked his mother

'Of course we're not going to eat you!'

'Eat me or you lose the bet.'

'We did it for a whole week and now you're just changing the rules.'

'*Eat me*!' shouted Gilbert.

'No!' wailed his mother.

'No!' screamed his dad. And that was that. Now both of them had refused to eat what was on their plates.

Which was exactly when Tinkerbell's magic went to work.

***

In a slivering silver flash the gleaming knives sprang up from the table and chopped their food into bite-sized pieces. Then to Mr and Mrs Sparrow's complete and utter horror, their forks shoved their son morsel by morsel down their gagging throats!

Do you believe in fairies *now*? You should do, because fairies are all around you. It's them what steals socks out of washing machines so that they can get a sniff of what you smell like. Then – should they ever need to teach you a lesson – they can smell where you are. Ever wondered why you sometimes wake up with a sore throat? That's a fairy paying you back for saying rude things to your mum and dad.

GED BE AHT O' 'ERE

That's Popering. He hasn't got a sore throat. He's just got his foot in his mouth.

You're going to like your cabin. You might find your towel gets a bit damp, but to be honest that'll be the least of your problems when the moray eels attack.

Now, there are many types of tales; tall tales, small tales, fairy tales and scary tales, but there are very few long tales. This is because readers fall asleep before they are finished. This tale, however, is very long, only NOT in the length department. I know it's confusing, but the length in this tale comes from distance between the top of the nose and the tip of the chin of a girl called Petula, or Petty as she was more commonly called. If such a distance can be measured by the span of a hand, on a normal person's face it measures one and a half. On Petula's face it was two hands and sometimes three! That is some length. A horse with its long pointed nose only measures five!

Take this poo away!

Do you think I've got a long face?

There do be dragons

I'll scream till I'm sick!

GED BE AHT O' 'ERE

Pump me up. I'm going down again

THE LONG FACE

There was a good reason why Petty had such a long face. She was a sulker; a huffer and puffer; a permanent pouter; a petulant princess whose stroppy bottom jaw jutted out so far that her face resembled a crescent moon. She lived in a castle in the country which was so big it was marked on Ordnance Survey maps with a pound sign to indicate that the owners, her parents, were wallowing in wonga. It was called Biddlethorpe Hall. Standing in three hundred acres of prime English countryside it came complete with its own lake, its own riding stables and its own haunted wood where the ghost of a headless horseman was said to butcher passing ramblers for their heads.

They should have kept an eye out for him . . . and given him that instead!

Petty's parents, Lord and Lady Ggambrel-Ffetlock were distant people. Both of them had been born in India at a time when doing things for yourself was unheard of. As a result they had unusual ideas about the rearing of children, believing that hard work, itchy clothes and cold bedrooms produced a well-behaved child who would not embarrass you at the golf club.

But somewhere something went wrong, because despite their strict rules Petty was *not* well-behaved and embarrassed them buckets. She knew every trick in the Big Book of Sulking to keep her parents twisted round her little finger: refusing to answer their questions, sneering at them in public, and turning her head away from a bedtime kiss. Not forgetting the daily exhibition of foot-stamping, curl-tossing and door-slamming. She was a master of the Dark-Browed Arts and it all began and ended with Jill.

***

Jill was a girl with none of Petula's advantages. She lived in the valley below Biddlethorpe Hall and her parents both worked to pay the rent. Life was not especially hard for Jill, but what the family had they had earned, which meant that Jill *treasured* her possessions ... unlike Petty, of course. Both girls had been born on the same day, so despite their different backgrounds they were always compared to each other at school and across the gossip counter at the post office. Jill was good at everything; schoolwork, games and helping her mother around the house and this, combined with a sunny disposition and curly hair, made her the most popular girl in town. Petty, on the other hand, could not have been less popular had she been outed as a baby-eating ogre.

Baby-eating ogres are always popular with ME.

Her glowering features and quick temper saw to that. Little surprise, therefore, that Petty saw Jill as the competition, as the girl she had to beat ... at everything.

In the early days when they were at primary school Petty would hide Jill's art apron to get her into trouble.

'She must have lost it, Miss. Shall we all pull her hair?'

When they moved up to bigger school, she knocked ink over Jill's homework or chewed her pencil nib so she couldn't make notes during lessons.

They never actually shared a

birthday party, but Petty always invited Jill to hers, not out of kindness, but so that she could humiliate her in front of all her friends.

'Now then,' said the hypnotist, 'who wants to come up and be hypnotised?'

Petty raised her hand. 'Aha, the Birthday Girl!'

'No, not me,' she said, feigning generosity, 'I've had such a lovely birthday it wouldn't be fair if I was hypnotised as well. Let Jill have some fun. It's *her* birthday too.'

So Jill was hypnotised and Petty took advantage, making her rival do unspeakable things whilst spellbound. Things like picking a dog's nose and eating it, putting a jelly in her pants then putting her pants on her head, and washing her hair in congealed chip oil. And when the two girls competed for their Friendship Badge in the Brownies, Petty hid kippers in Jill's shoes. It took Brown Owl three days to find the source of the stink, by which time Jill had no friends left at all.

Pump me up. I'm going down again

That's just Ida deflating. Ignore her.

Lord and Lady Ggambrel-Ffetlock always knew if Petty was having a problem with Jill, because the sulks would go on for longer than usual.

'Why the long face now?' asked Lady Ggambrel-Ffetlock one evening after Petty had thrown her ravioli over Nanny Betty's head.

Petty grunted and turned her back on her mother. 'I hate it when you say that!'

'Say what?'

'About the long face.'

'You always have a long face.'

'No, I don't. It's a normal face.'

'Not when you're sulking, Petula. You seem unhappy.'

Petty stomped over to the bedroom window, plonked herself down on a bench and stared out at the sky. 'I am,' she snapped. 'But there's nothing you can do about it because you never buy me what I want.'

'You mean unlike the new four-poster bed you wanted three months ago, or the new mobile phone and MP3 player you wanted last week, or the Fashion House Dress Designer you wanted yesterday, or—'

'All right!' screamed the spoilt girl. 'I get the message, mother! You're fired,' she said to her

Fashion House Dress Designer. So he packed up his tulles and tartans and left.

Lady Ggambrel–Ffetlock sat down on Petty's bed and patted the duvet. 'Your father and I are flying to Vienna for the opera tonight,' she said, 'so either you tell me what is bothering you or you go to bed angry.'

'What's the point?' pouted Petty. 'You'll only say no.'

'Try me.'

'I want a pony!' she wailed. 'A winning pony that just wins and wins and wins and never stops.'

'But you can't ride,' said her mother.

'*See!*' squealed the girl. 'I said you'd say "no".'

'I haven't said anything!' protested her mother defensively.

'You haven't said "yes".'

'We'll discuss this in the morning when you're in a better mood.'

***

But in the morning the cloud over Petty's head was even darker. She refused to get out of bed so Lord Ggambrel-Ffetlock was separated from his devilled kidneys to explain to his daughter the need for obedience.

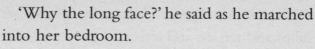

'Why the long face?' he said as he marched into her bedroom.

'Is that *all* you and Mother can say?' barked Petty from inside the folds of her duvet.

'No,' he said. 'I can also say this, Petula. Fathers are wiser than daughters, which is why what they say is always right and must be obeyed. Were it the other way round chaos would follow. And do we want chaos?'

'No. We want a pony,' muttered the girl.

'I'm glad we got on to that,' said her father. 'Why should you have a pony when you can't even look after a hamster?'

'That is *so* unfair!' she howled, exploding out of her duvet in a flurry of arms and hair. 'It wasn't my fault he had a nervous breakdown, thought he was a lemming and threw himself out of the window.'

'*You* threw him out of the window, Petula, in a fit of pique when I refused to buy you a crate of ghostly carrots so that you and Jill could go into the haunted wood to feed the headless horseman's horse.'

'You're so mean! I was going to give those carrots to Jill as a present, because she likes horses.'

'And no doubt scare her half to death when the horse turned up and its headless rider tried to cut her head off! There is something not nice about you, my girl.'

Which Petty took as a compliment.

What neither of her parents could winkle out of their daughter was *why* she wanted a pony. It should have been obvious. Jill had been given one. It was called Crumble, had a tufty coat of butterscotch brown, a mane of platinum white, a warm, pink nose and long, soft eyelashes that brushed Jill's cheek whenever she stroked its face. They were a brilliant team. In fact they had won every gymkhana in the county. Jill had a mantelpiece brimming with trophies and Crumble's stable door was covered in rosettes.

***

For three long days Petty put her parents to the sword with a sulk of professional proportions. The house sighed with her heavy silence and shook as her boots dented the furniture. In fact, it was the longest time she'd ever had such a long face and eventually, after the fourth silent breakfast on the trot, it paid off. Lord and Lady Ggambrel-Ffetlock made a secret dash to the horse shop and bought their precious angel not just a pony, but all the trimmings as well – saddle, tack, straw, brushes, feed bag, biscuits, toothbrush and ribbons for its mane.

'Not hard to see the attraction of goldfish, is it?' grumbled Lord Ggambrel–Ffetlock as he stood at the cash till and paid the huge bill.

Luckily it wasn't a big pony so they were able to get it home in the back of the car and sneak it into the stable without Petty seeing. When they told her that there was a surprise for her in the courtyard, she ran downstairs whooping with excitement. But when she saw the pony she stopped in her tracks.

'Did you ask the pony shop man if it was the best, because I said I only wanted the best? You heard me say that didn't you? I said I only wanted a winner.'

'Don't you think it's a beautiful pony?' asked Lady Ggambrel–Ffetlock.

'It's a bit small,' was her long-faced daughter's reply.

'What are you going to call it?'

'I wasn't going to call it anything.'

'You've got to give it a name,' exclaimed Petty's mother.

'If I give it a name I will get attached to it and that's not why I've got it. I don't want to *love* it. I'm going to learn to ride and then go out and beat Jill at gymkhanas!'

'That's all very well,' said Lady Ggambrel-Ffetlock. 'But who's going to teach you?'

'Hopefully the same person who's looking after it,' said Petty.

Her father's jaw dropped open. 'I thought *you'd* be looking after it,' he gasped.

'*Me!*' sniggered Petty. 'Look after *that* smelly thing! I'd rather die. You have to get me a groom who can look after the horse, prepare it for competition and teach me how to ride.'

'A groom!' he exploded.

'Yes, a horse-servant. Sleeps in the stable, on damp straw. You must have heard of a groom.'

And when her father said, 'Impossible!' Petula Ggambrel-Ffetlock pushed out her lower jaw, folded her arms, sat on the floor and growled.

There do be dragons

There do be doo-bee-doo-bee-doo-bee-doo as well. Josiah, but you're not watching it.

Nine hours later, she had herself a groom. His name was Stuart Piddle, but she called him Stu Pid, because she said that suited him best. He had a big head on a scrawny body which made him the ideal size for a jockey. He loved horses and knew everything about them, not that Petty cared about that.

'So,' he said when he first arrived, 'you'll obviously be wanting the welfare of the animal to come first at all times. I'll be mucking out the stable twice a day, sterilising the bit, getting him shod and wormed and jabbed by the vet. Don't want him going lame. What have you got to feed him?'

'I'm not bothered with food,' said Petty. 'I don't care if his fur is matted and he's got flies in his ears

just so long as he jumps fences and beats Jill.'

'He won't perform if he's not looked after.'

'Then see to it that he *is*!' she glowered, thumping Stu between his shoulders to make her point.

'OK,' he said reluctantly. 'And what shall I call him?'

'Dog Food,' said Petty proudly, 'because that's what he'll be if he doesn't win!'

> In an amusing twist of fate, dog food's all Petty can eat nowadays.

While Jill continued to pick up trophies, Petty made Stu get up at four o'clock every morning to put Dog Food through his paces. She checked up on them before breakfast and again in the middle of the morning, and if she felt that they weren't making enough progress she would take a whip to the horse and demand more effort. And when Stu grabbed the cane and told her to stop, she wrenched it out of his grip and beat *him* with it too.

Once the pony was tamed, Petty climbed aboard and told Stu to teach her all he knew about riding.

'Because,' she informed him, 'I shall be riding on Sunday in the last gymkhana of the season, and I intend to win.'

'You'll never do that!' he said. 'It takes months of practice to jump over fences. You could hurt yourself, not to mention the horse.'

'Then *don't* mention it,' she said. 'Now where do I start? Hup!' And she swung her legs across the pony's neck and kicked it in the eye.

She was hopeless. When he told her to grip with her knees she complained that it hurt her back and when he asked her to rise and fall in the saddle she looked at him with a gimlet eye that would have withered tree bark. 'It's bruising my bum,' she said. 'No!'

***

Come Sunday at the gymkhana, therefore, she was woefully unprepared. Before the jumping Dog Meat was admired by the judges for being so beautifully presented, but when it came to the competition success was more elusive. The little pony did its best, but it was carrying a dead weight around on its back — a sulky lump of a girl who didn't like riding and kept whispering, 'Come on, Dog Meat, do it for your mistress or it's the heat-sealed can for you!' which rather put him off his stride. He knocked down three fences, which as far as Petty was concerned was three fences too many, especially when Jill and Crumble came first again, and afterwards Jill kissed Dog Meat's long nose and told Petty that she had a lovely pony and one day he was sure to win something. That comment, as far as Petty was concerned, was rubbing salt into the wound.

Now that IS a good torture. It stings like billio — but not as much as mustard.

When she got home she was in a funk to end all funks. She hated it when she didn't get her own way, and this time it was the fault of this stupid pony!

'Why the long face?' asked her mother when Petty refused to get out of the car.

'Stop saying that!' exploded the grumpy girl. 'I haven't got a long face.'

'It looks long enough to ski off,' commented her father.

'It's all *your* fault,' she screamed. 'I knew it was a bad idea to buy him!'

'Who?' said her mother.

'Dog Meat.' She kicked open the car door and stepped out into the courtyard. 'I'm going to get rid of him.' Her parents shot out of opposite doors and grabbed an arm each.

'No,' said her mother. 'Petula, you can't.'

'Stop telling me what I can do,' threatened Petty, shaking herself free. 'And when I've done it, if I hear one word of a telling off I shall sulk you into your graves, both of you!' Then she stomped off leaving Lord and Lady Ggambrel-Ffetlock shipwrecked in a sea of despair.

'I don't know what else we can do,' sobbed Petty's mother.

'We can leave her alone,' said her husband, 'and let her learn the hard way.'

Is there any other way to teach a child?

Petty told Stu to take Dog Meat to the Pet Food factory.

'If he can't beat Crumble he's no good to me!' she said. 'He needs punishing. Get them to grind up his bones really small!'

'No,' said Stu. 'I can't do that.'

'You *can* and you *will*!' she replied, frothing from the corners of her mouth like an agitated racehorse. She picked up her swishing cane and cracked it across the groom's back. 'I can do what I like to both of you!' She chased the boy and the pony from the stable. 'And don't think I won't know if you've lied to me,' she shouted. 'If you come back here and tell me he's canned when he's not, I'll have *you* turned into pet food too!'

Now Stuart Piddle may have been a simple lad,

but he was *not* stupid, and more than anything else he could not bear cruelty to animals. He could no more lead Dog Meat to the slaughterhouse than cut off his own thumb. As he walked away from Biddlethorpe Hall on the path to the village he passed the entrance to the haunted wood. The trunks of the silver larch trees glistened white like scrubbed bones. Their branches stretched out across the forest floor like long, thin fingers and entwined with others to create a latticed web of secrecy. Ten metres off the path and the wood screened its heart from passing eyes. What better place to hide a pony? Behind the barrier of silver larch Dog Meat would become invisible, and even if he *was* seen, nobody dared enter the wood for fear of the headless horseman! Leading the pony by the reins, Stu guided it through the tree-line into the dappled interior, where he left it to graze on wild mushrooms. Then he turned back to Biddlethorpe Hall with a lie on his lips to convince his mistress that her pony had passed into pet food.

Imagine his surprise, therefore, when he emerged from the wood to find his mistress standing there tapping her foot.

'I knew you'd betray me,' spat the girl with the long, sulky face. 'Small people with big heads can't help being deceitful. Now you're going to pay!' As she cracked her cane across his shoulder blades Stu garbled a lie to save his skin.

'I was just coming to get you,' he cried. 'The pony got a stone in its hoof and went lame, and I knew it wouldn't reach the pet food factory, so I tied it up in the wood, where it wouldn't wander off and was just coming back to get the car.'

'You're *lying*,' she snarled. 'I followed you. I watched you look around before you went into the trees. The pony wasn't lame and you looked shifty.' She plunged into the clutch of silver larches brushing aside the wooden fingers. The groom gave chase, blurting out nonsense in the hope that she would leave the pony alone.

'He needs a blacksmith. If you want to help you should go back home and phone one.'

By now she was beside the pony. She lashed out with her whip and watched it jump nimbly out of the way. 'Doesn't seem injured to me,' she said.

'No …' said Stuart Piddle. 'I mean yes … I mean …' Having run out of lies the groom had nowhere else to go but the truth. 'You're cruel,' he said. 'You and that ugly long face of yours should be taught to behave properly.'

'How *dare* you,' she yelled. 'I don't have a long face!'

'Yes you do,' he said. 'On a horse it would look beautiful, but not on you!'

Just then the birds stopped singing and in the distance a patter of hooves ate up the forest floor. Petty and Stu stopped talking and cocked their ears to the sound of a horse galloping closer. It crashed through fallen branches and kicked up clods of earth. The blood drained from their faces as they realised what was coming.

'I want to go home now,' whimpered Petty Ggambrel-Ffetlock. 'Take me home immediately.'

But Stuart Piddle was rooted to the spot. 'We're not going anywhere,' he whispered as the thunder rolled out of the forest.

'It can't be!' screeched the girl.

'It is,' said the boy.

The Headless Horseman's horse, a black steed with smoking breath, soared over a fallen tree as its master drew his sword. With one clean slice he swished the blade through the groom's scrawny neck cutting his head clean off. It somersaulted in

46

midair and landed bloody-side up in the phantom's lap with eyelids cold and still. Petty had forgotten to breathe. She watched in stifled horror as her groom's headless body bounced off the ground like a bag of straw. The ghost then lifted Stu's head and pressed it down upon his own jagged neck. The eyes sprang open as the ghostly blood flowed through its veins.

'And now for you!' said the Headless Horseman in a voice that matched Stuart Piddle's in every rhythm and tone.

'What are you going to do to me?' stammered the terrified girl.

'Before I was headless I was a blacksmith,' said the apparition with a crooked smile. 'Let's see if I've still got my skills.' Then he jumped down from his horse and unrolled the iron instruments of his trade from a sack attached to his saddle – a hammer, a pair of pincers, a punch for making rivet holes and a poker, for which he had no other purpose than red hot fun.

***

When Petty woke up she was lying on the ground, alone. The ghostly blacksmith with the head of her groom, his black horse and her little pony had gone. She looked across to where Stuart Piddle's body had landed, but that had been cleared away. On the forest floor next to her right hand, the Headless Horseman had left a looking glass and a note scrawled hastily in blood . . .

In future when people ask you 'Why the long face?' you must tell them. 'Because I'm a horse.'

Scared of what she might see, she hesitated as she picked up the mirror and moved it reluctantly towards her face. When it came into view she screamed, only screaming was not as easy as it had once been, because the lower part of her face had been reconstructed with iron bars. The bones had been broken and lengthened by the insertion of an external metal frame welded to her skull. It had elongated her face from the top of her nose to the tip of her chin, so that now she looked every inch a horse.

***

'Oh there you are,' said Lady Ggambrel–Ffetlock when her daughter sheepishly entered the dining room for supper that night. 'Where've you been?'

'And why the long face?' asked her father.

'Gego I'g a gor,' she said, or rather *didn't* say because her jaw didn't move. In fact, she didn't say much from then on, which made everyone's life considerably more tolerable.

As for Jill, she carried on winning gymkhanas and when she grew up she won a gold medal for Britain in the Olympic Games. Sadly, not on a pony called Dog Food. He and the ghostly groom paired up and entered gymkhanas all over the country.
Unfortunately they're still looking for their first win on account of one tiny technical flaw. Whenever the little pony goes over a jump its rider's head falls off.

Talking of Dog Food. I love anything in a tin, because the serrated lids make lethal Frisbees if you hurl them into a crowded bathroom. It' amuses me to see what drops off.

Pump me up. I'm going down again

That girl's doing my head in. I put a special bed of nails in her cabin and she's in my earhole 24/7.

Where was I? Oh yes – Josiah. On the West coast of Cornwall, jutting into the wild sea like a gnarled dragon's claw is a rocky promontory called The End of the World.

It is not the literal end of the world; for *that* you have to travel to Finland, take a left at Reykavik and keep walking for fifteen hundred miles until you fall off the edge. No, The End of the World is only called The End of the World because it looks like it.

Here, the sea smashes its angry fists into the rocks with such ferocity that there is nothing beyond the shoreline, but death. Many a stone-cold smuggler can testify to that. Standing tall amidst the clamour and white spume that flicks off the tops of the waves like camel spit is an extraordinary sight; a bony white finger raised in defiance at the sea. For three hundred years this lighthouse blinked its fiery eye into the darkness and saved sailors' lives, then in 1997 its gas burner was extinguished and the crumbling white tower was condemned to demolition, except that when the demolition men turned up with their wrecking balls they found a sign nailed to the wooden door. Its message struck such fear in their hearts that they turned tail and ran away as fast as their chicken feet would carry them. That night the light came back on, and every night since it has cast its man-made moon across the water. Nobody knows who's in there, and nobody dares go in to find out. What are they scared of? Is it the thumping din of rotor blades that drowns out the waves, the giant winged shadow that stretches out across the sea; or that sign on the door? HERE BE DRAGONS.

THE DRAGON MOTH

Even before Josiah Reeks was born his parents knew he was going to be trouble. They were having a barbecue in the garden when Mr Reeks pointed up at the sky.

'Are those clouds trying to tell us something?' he said.

Mrs Reeks shielded her eyes from the sun and gasped. 'They're spelling out a sentence,' she replied. 'It says ... *Oy You! Yes, You With The Babby In Yore Tummy. Give This Child Away To A Travling Circus. He is Trubble.*'

'Clouds are not very good spellers, are they?' said Mr Reeks, rather missing the point. 'I could spell better than that.' This gave him an idea and the following day he started a new career as a sign writer. Anyway, the point was that Mr and Mrs Reeks should have heeded the warning sign in the sky, but didn't, and because it led directly to Mr Reeks becoming a sign writer, which in turn led to Josiah becoming a rebel, they had only themselves to blame. At least that's what Josiah wanted them to think. Putting the blame for his own disobedience onto his parents kept them just where he wanted them – under his thumb.

*****

Every day at breakfast he was required to eat his toast. He knew this, because there was a sign on the table saying **EAT YOUR TOAST**. So every morning he devised a different way to defy the sign. He tossed the toast into the washing up bowl or crumbled it onto the floor for the mice, or shoved three pieces into his mouth at once and chewed with his mouth open.

'That is disgusting!' squealed Mrs Reeks.

'Shall I spit it out then?' sniggered the cunning boy who knew she'd say that.

'No!' she wailed. 'Why can't you do as you're told?'

'It's not my fault!' he mumbled, splattering his parents with crusty spit. 'I live in a house surrounded by signs. I can't breathe for instructions.

BRUSH YOUR TEETH; DON'T RUN ON THE STAIRS; SWITCH THAT LIGHT OFF! Is it any wonder that occasionally I need to spread my wings and fly against the wind?'

'They're only harmless signs,' said his father. 'I used to read them to you instead of a bedtime story. You can't tell me bedtime stories are bad for you.'

'That's the problem,' shouted Josiah. 'Most children are read Enid Blyton and Roald Dahl, but I get **TAKE CARE. SLIPPERY PAVEMENT** and **DANGER! MEN AT WORK!**' By now his mouth was crammed with so much toast that the brown bulge between his lips looked like the backside of a bear reversing out of a small cave. 'If you didn't put ideas in my head with your stupid signs, I'd be a good boy, I would.'

'But the whole point of my signs,' Mr Reeks exclaimed, picking up the one he had only recently finished for the Chimpanzee's cage at London Zoo **– PLEASE DO NOT LAUGH AT THE CHIMPS WHEN THEY SPIT OUT THEIR FOOD. IT ONLY ENCOURAGES THEM –** 'is to tell people what they *shouldn't* be doing.'

'Oh, is that right?' smirked Josiah, spitting bits of toast all over the table. 'They always make me do the opposite.'

> In which case I'd write a sign saying DO NOT PUT YOUR HEAD IN THIS MINCING MACHINE

The truth was, it wasn't his father's signs that made him do the opposite. Josiah was contrary from birth. Less than an hour after he was born he had already disobeyed the signs in the hospital corridor. Instead of being QUIET he screamed so loudly that the nurses told his mother to take him home. The fact that he *stopped* screaming the second he left the building should have told his parents that he was playing them for fools, but it didn't. And so it went on. The day he learned to walk, he walked to the park, walked across the grass and stole all of the **DO NOT WALK ON THE GRASS** signs; on his first day at nursery school he took one look at the sign on the back of the loo door – **NOW WASH YOUR HANDS** – and washed his feet instead; and the first time he was confronted by the sign in the newsagent's window that said **ONLY TWO SCHOOLCHILDREN AT A TIME** he phoned up every child at school and invited them into the shop for a *Help-Yourself-To-As-Many-Sweets-As-You-Can-Stuff-Down-Your-Trousers* party.

As a rule, the children who lived in this Cornish seaside village were *well*-behaved. This was because of the cliffs overlooking the End of the World and the local schoolteacher, Old Nudger Nicholson, having a special liking for pushing pupils off.

He taught me.

So being *badly*-behaved, Josiah stuck out like a sore thumb. His disobedience started off harmlessly enough when he discovered that if he ran into the playground through the gate marked GIRLS he got the same reaction every time.

'Get out! Get out! Get out!' screeched the girls. 'You're *not* a girl, Josiah! You're the owner of a dangly prawn and you make our lovely entrance gate smell like a dustbin!'

But as he grew older, small transgressions became bigger and more dangerous. Getting his finger stuck up his nose after opening a tube of Superglue clearly labelled – **DO NOT PICK YOUR NOSE AFTER HANDLING GLUE**; getting trapped in the fridge after ignoring the magnetic sign on the door – **DO NOT EVEN THINK OF HIDING IN THIS FRIDGE.** His parents despaired and begged him to stop disobeying signs.

'Why should I?' he sniffed defiantly. 'I disobey signs and never get punished. The reason signs are so boring is because they are always trying to protect us from things that never happen.'

'That's not true,' said his father, hurt by his son's low opinion of his profession. 'Signs contain wisdom passed down from generation to generation.'

'You mean like **HOT DOGS SOLD HERE?**' sneered Josiah. 'Very wise.'

'Don't be so horrid to your father,' snapped Mrs Reeks. 'Signs are there to keep you safe! Ignore them at your peril!'

'OK,' said Josiah with a mischievous glint in his eye, 'if signs are there to protect me, that means dragons must exist.'

The mention of dragons came out of the blue and struck Mr and Mrs Reeks like a double blow from a scythe. His mother laughed brittly, in a failed attempt to convince her son that nothing was wrong.

'What are you talking about?' she trilled.

Josiah could see that he had their attention.

'Well, at school today,' he explained, 'Old Nudger

Nicholson said there's a sign on the lighthouse door that says, **HERE BE DRAGONS.'** His parent's eyebrows flickered. 'That's one sign I'd like to see.'

'Never,' growled his father. 'That is one sign you will *never* see!'

'So you *are* scared there might be dragons up there then?' It was a subject Josiah's father did not wish to discuss so he kept his answer brief.

'A child went missing a few years ago, then another last year. They'd both gone to the lighthouse. They trawled the sea for the bodies, but found nothing. To this day nobody knows what became of them.'

'Stop it,' interrupted Mrs Reeks. 'You're scaring him. Dragons don't exist, Josiah. The reason we don't want you going up there is because the lighthouse isn't safe. Something might fall on your head.'

'I don't believe you,' said Josiah.

'You don't have to,' growled his father. 'You just have to do as you're told.'

***

But, of course, Josiah never did as he was told and being told *not* to go to the lighthouse simply fuelled his desire to get there.

I'LL SCREAM TILL I'M SICK!

Be my guest, Vicky. Only remember; the bag's already full. One more puke and I'll have to put you out for the dustbin-fish.

***

Later that night, when Mr and Mrs Reeks tucked their son up in bed, Mr Reeks placed a freshly painted sign on the end of Josiah's bed – **DO NOT GO TO THE LIGHTHOUSE.**

'To remind you in the morning,' he explained. Then they kissed their son on the forehead and left. As Josiah sat up, a moth flew in through the open window, fluttered up to the lightbulb and cast a giant shadow across the wall.

'Right,' said the boy, tossing back his duvet to reveal that he was already dressed. 'To the lighthouse!' Then he swung his legs out of bed, climbed out of the window and slid silently down the drainpipe.

There was only one way to find the End of the World in the dark. Slipping through a hole in the fence, past three explicit warning signs – **NO**

TRESPASSING, ELECTRICITY KILLS and **DANGER TRAINS** – Josiah slid down the embankment and ran in a straight line, following the glint of the moon on the railway tracks. Half a mile further on as the track disappeared into a tunnel, Josiah climbed up the bank towards the sound of the sea. He ducked under some barbed wire and ran across a field peppered with mossy boulders, in the far corner of which was the deserted lighthouse, glowing white in the darkness like a boiled bone.

The lighthouse was surrounded by a broken picket fence. Josiah pushed through the gate ignoring a sign that said **NO ENTRY. PRIVATE PROPERTY.** Now that he was closer to the building he could see that somebody had covered the walls in graffiti. Hundreds of messages blocked out in red paint. **KEEP OUT. COME NO CLOSER. GO HOME. STAY AWAY IF YOU KNOW WHAT'S GOOD FOR YOU** and Josiah's favourite because it was written in ten-foot-high letters and had an exclamation mark, **BEGONE!** What made these signs strange, though, apart from the quantity of them, was that each warning was followed by the most terrifying word of all. **JOSIAH!**

Of course, any normal person would have taken

the hint and rushed home before whatever it was inside the lighthouse that wanted to *protect* its privacy came out and *defended* it. But Josiah wasn't normal.

He was a Gnaughty Gnome of 'No!'

Twice he circled the building looking for a way in, but couldn't find a door. Then all of a sudden above his head a loose shutter clattered into the brickwork. He glanced up, spray stinging his cheeks, and there he saw it. Six feet off the ground, cut into the side of the lighthouse like a button hole, the door, and hanging from a nail hammered into the wood, the sign, **HERE BE DRAGONS.**

Suddenly, there was a noise from inside the lighthouse, a throbbing din of rotor blades as if a helicopter had started up. At the same time Josiah heard a crackle of electricity and the thump of a gas flame being lit, then the light at the top of the lighthouse came on. Its beam pierced the darkness like a white stiletto and flashed off the tips of the waves below. Josiah's feet had frozen to the ground. What in the name of The Devil was that huge

shadow stretched out across the sea?
As it arched its long neck and
flapped its gargantuan wings Josiah
knew the answer. It was the beast
awake in its lair!

Now maybe for once he would
heed the warning signs, do as he was told and
begone!

But even as Josiah made his decision to flee, the
door creaked open and swung back against the wall.
The boy's fearful eyes were drawn towards the
opening, waiting for the dragon's scaly face to
appear with its child-chomping teeth and fireball-
snorting nostrils. Instead a moth flew out. Josiah
laughed with relief.

'A moth!' he roared. 'A little-itty-bitty moth!
What a cast-iron fool I am. That big flapping
shadow on the sea wasn't a dragon at all, it was a
moth fluttering in front of the lighthouse's powerful
lamp!'

Now that his fear had vanished it amused him.
He took his eyes off the open door. 'I know what
you are,' he shouted at the warning signs scribbled
on the lighthouse walls. 'You've been put up there
by smugglers to scare people away. They've got
stolen gold and whisky hidden in this lighthouse.

What better way to keep people from snooping around than by telling them there's a dragon living here!'

Now that there was nothing to be scared of anymore and the prospect of finding gold inside, Josiah turned his attention back to the door and the problem of how he was going to get up to it. He was, however, no longer alone. Standing on the threshold was a bearded old man wearing a brown and green leather patchwork suit which made him look like a snake. On his head he wore a miner's hat with a light on the front and over his shoulders a fiery red cape.

'Josiah Reeks!' he whispered in a soft voice that caught the wind and travelled directly into the boy's ear. 'I am the dragonmaster. The dragon performs at my will. Begone, young warrior, and I shall keep the beast at bay.'

Josiah was not falling for any of this theatre. 'I know what you're up to,' he said. 'You're the smuggler, trying to get rid of me so you can stash some more booty.'

The dragonmaster carried on as if Josiah hadn't spoken. 'When the dragon is hungry I can hold it no longer. Leave now. Obey my signs and you will be spared.' Josiah sat down as the old man placed another sign on the door. Under **HERE BE DRAGONS** it now read **AND HERE BE DEATH TOO.**

'I'm not going,' said the boy haughtily, 'until I've had a look inside.'

The dragonmaster did not reply. He turned back through the open door and brought out a wooden ladder which he leant against the door step 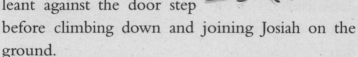 before climbing down and joining Josiah on the ground.

Up close, Josiah could see that the old man's face was a bag of wrinkles. He pressed a finger to his lips to indicate that Josiah should stop talking, then took out a notepad and pencil and wrote down a message. **KEEP YOUR VOICE DOWN. IT CAN HEAR YOU.** Then he added in a secret whisper, 'I'm not really the dragonmaster. I'm the dragon's *slave*, empowered to find it food whenever it wakes.'

'I don't believe you,' said the boy.

'Quiet!' urged the old man. 'You woke it when you came through the gate and brushed past the **NO ENTRY** sign. It smelled your blood and now it's angry and wants to sup it. Go home. Save your skin.'

But the belligerent boy who never did as he was told, pushed past the old man, and strode to the foot of the ladder.

'Dragon!' he cried. 'If you really exist come out and face me!' He looked back at the old man who had swapped his look of concern for a broad smile.

'I did try to warn you,' he said, 'but you wouldn't listen. Just as I predicted.'

'Predicted?' said Josiah. 'What do you mean?'

'Like I said, you silly boy, I am the dragon's slave empowered to deliver him food. That is why I painted all these signs on the lighthouse to catch bad children like you, Josiah; to lure you to the lighthouse as food for my master.'

'You mean the dragon really exists?'

'Not a dragon, no, but a dragon moth – a colossus of a bug nurtured these last ten years by the brilliant lamp of the lighthouse, grown big and strong by the warmth of the giant bulb.'

Josiah blinked. 'Are you saying that you only told me to flee because you knew I would stay?'

'Bullseye!' cackled the old man. 'You Gnomes of 'No!' are all the same; always do the opposite to what you're asked. And now that you are still here and not at home where you should be, let dinner begin!'

***

As he spoke the dragon moth emerged from the lighthouse. It was ten metres long with antennae like bullwhips and wings that unfurled like the sails of the merchant ships that smugglers wrecked on the rocks. As the leviathan lumbered into the sky Josiah suddenly wished that he had paid heed to the painted signs warning him of danger, but it was too late for that. The down-draught from the beast's beating wings bore down on his back as he took to his heels and ran back across the field, dodging from boulder to boulder as the giant moth thrummed overhead. With one lunge it grabbed Josiah by the neck of his shirt and lifted him into the air. The boy struggled but there was no breaking the insect's grip. It carried him off to The End of the World and dropped him onto the rocks, where his skull split in two like a clam shell and spilled his delicious brain into a foaming red sea.

If only the signs had said; STAY HERE AND GET EATEN BY A DRAGON MOTH. Josiah Reeks would still be alive today, but then the dragon moth would still have been hungry and still have needed feeding. It still does, in fact, twice a year. Who knows – maybe its next supper is **you!**

---

is the Dragon's next supper me?
An exciting Quiz

Question 1: Read this sign out loud ·
DO NOT READ THIS SIGN OUT LOUD

Answer: YES. Go take a bath in Garlic Butter

I expect you're wondering how Josiah came to be aboard the Pain and Everlasting Torment when a giant moth had gobbled him up? Simple, really. Even moths have got to go. And this one went over the sea, so he floated down to me as a lump of pongy guano. I keep him on a cheese board at the Captain's Table to remind me of the cheese which I love and what I can't get for love nor money underwater. Have you ever tried milking a swordfish? Don't. It hurts.

Pump me up. I'm going down again

If balloon-girl asks me again I'm going to blow her up for good — with two sticks of dynamite!

The next tale starts way back in the mists of time, a time when men wore jockstraps made from buffalo fur and women grew their hair long so that they wouldn't have to walk to the shops, because their men-folk could drag them there. We're talking about prehistoric times, of course, when woolly mammoths appeared on Christmas cards and takeaways did a roaring trade in Veloceraptor Wraps. It was also a primitive time for speech. Language was limited to grunts and screams. So, for example, a conversation between a young girl and her mother, in which the young girl wanted her mother to buy her a fashionable blueberry juice stick for her lips and her mother refused, might have gone something like this.

'Aaaaaaaaaaaaagh!' (I want it I want it I want it!)

'Ug!' (You can't have it.)

'Aaaaaaaaaaaaagh!' (But I want it I want it I want it!)

'Ug!' (You're too young for make-up)

'**Aaaaaaaaaaaaagh!**' (That's so unfair!)

'**Ug!**' (Life isn't fair, Mfannwy. You only have to see what happened to your younger brother last week when he was eaten by that sabre tooth tiger.)

'**Aaaaaaaaaaaaagh!**' (I hate you!)

'**Ug!**' (I know. One day you'll have the same conversation with your daughter.)

'**Aaaaaaaaaaaaagh!**' (I'm going to my room to play some rocks music. I don't ever want to talk to you again!)

'**Ug!**' (Did I tell you that granny's coming on Sunday?)

Let us now travel forward in time to a period of undoubted civilisation, but still backward in so many ways. And it was only fifty years ago.

SICK TO DEATH

Can you believe that there was a time *without* upright vacuum cleaners; a time when brushes did the cleaning, sold door-to-door by ambitious young men in shapeless suits; a time when women wore skirts that flared from the waist like lampshades and stayed at home to clean and cook and wash dishes by hand; a time when computers were the size of double-decker buses; a time when there was no TV and reading books was the most popular form of entertainment; a time when children died of chicken pox and flu, and cats and dogs were eaten on Sundays with vegetables grown in the piles of steaming horse manure that lined the highways and byways of the British Empire?

It was at such a time that Victoria Spew (known as Sicky Vicky to her friends) reached the difficult age of eleven. To be frank, every age from one upwards had been difficult for Victoria, because Victoria was a difficult child. Her father was one of the young men in shapeless suits who sold brushes door-to-door and despite the fact that he was away all week, Victoria worshipped him, because at weekends he spoiled his little princess with silver and tortoise-shell gifts from his brush collection. But his absence meant that Victoria spent most of her childhood alone in the house with her mother, which meant that she could treat her mother like a servant and get away with it. She demanded her full co-operation in everything she wanted to do, and if her mother refused, Victoria would scream until she was sick; a fountain of pink soup every time she didn't get her own way. It was a successful recipe she'd worked out over a number of years.

Take one unreasonable demand.

'I shan't be going to school today.'

Add one parental order.

'I think you will, Victoria, dear.'

Mix in a six decibel scream.

'Aaaaaaaaaaaaaagh!'

And top it all off with a tantrumic tummy chunder, preferably over Mummy's carpet and all down her patent leather shoes. Then serve it up six times a day for ten years until your mother is at her wits' end and can't be bothered to fight you any more.

One other factor played into Victoria's hands. Mrs Spew was a woman with a weak constitution. The very sight of sick made her feel queasy, which meant that when she was required to clean it up she couldn't. She left the puddles for Mr Spew to do when he came home at the weekend which, as you can imagine, was not the most pleasant of jobs, and when he complained, she always informed him in a brisk, matronly tone:

'You are the most suitable man in the world to clean up sick, Mr Spew. After all, your job is to demonstrate the cleaning properties of brushes and what better place to practise your skills than at home.'

Poor Mr Spew – away all week and up to his elbows in vomit at the weekend.

The point is that in the Spew household language had not progressed much beyond the Stone Age.

The daughter was still screaming to get what she wanted and the mother still wasn't listening. It was a shocking state of affairs.

***

Then, one Saturday after supper, Victoria threw down her knife and fork and burst into crocodile tears.

'Oh, Daddy,' she cried, fluttering her moist eyes, 'have I done something to upset you? Is that why you haven't given me a present this weekend?'

Mr Spew grimaced with embarrassment. 'The thing is, princess, Daddy's work's a little bit difficult at the moment. I don't want you to worry yourself, brushes *are* still popular, but not quite as popular as they once were.'

Victoria's face turned white with shock. 'You mean you *haven't* got me a present, because you're too—' the word froze on her lips. '—poor?' she shrieked. 'But you *always* bring me one!'

'Victoria!' Mrs Spew was outraged at her daughter's selfish outburst. 'How dare you speak to your father like that. If he says he hasn't got you a present you don't ask him why!'

Now that her mother had intervened Victoria stopped trying to be saccharine sweet and took off like a flying bomb.

'So what are you saying, Mummy? That I'm *wrong* to want a present? I'm a child. It's what we do. And I shall scream and scream until I get one!' The she took a deep breath and started screaming.

'Stop it,' yelled her father, who seemed unusually tense. 'I can't take it anymore!' His hands, which were still red raw from scrubbing the sick off the floor that morning, were shaking.

'*You* can't take it anymore!' spat Mrs Spew, joining the fray with gusto. 'You're not the one who has to live with the stink all week.'

'No, but I'm the one who has to clear it up,' he snarled, raising his voice to make himself heard above Victoria's scream.

'I keep telling you,' she pushed on, 'I *can't* clear up sick. It's not in my nature and if that is a problem buy me one of those new-fangled upright vacuum cleaners. In the advertisements it says it even sucks up liquids.'

'What?' gasped Mr Spew.

'A vacuum cleaner. Our house need never smell

of sick again.'

'A vacuum cleaner? The Devil's own household appliance?'

Say what you will, but I can't see The Devil flicking round Hell with a feather duster.

'Oh don't be so over-dramatic,' jeered Mrs Spew as Victoria's screaming face turned an angry shade of scarlet.

'How can you even *mention* that thing in my presence?' he gasped. 'The upright vacuum cleaner is killing the brush trade. Before long nobody will want brushes anymore and then I'll be out of a job!'

'Then make the switch now. Start selling vacuum cleaners,' suggested his wife, who was practical in all things save sick disposal.

'*SELL VACUUM CLEANERS!*' exploded Mr Spew. 'Vacuum cleaners are sold by spivs and charlatans! There is more honour in selling the teeth out of dead bodies than selling vacuum cleaners!'

'A vacuum cleaner salesman rang on our doorbell the other day,' she said provocatively. 'He seemed quite nice.'

Mr Spew bristled like a fighting cockerel. 'Was he friendly?' he hissed.

'Very,' she smiled. 'He said it was a shame that a pretty woman like me had to live in a house that smelled of sick.'

'And what was *he* going to do about it?' fumed Mr Spew.

'He said that an upright vacuum cleaner would be the answer to all my problems. Not only would it suck up the pink puddles so that my husband wouldn't have to clean them up at the weekend, but it would stop Victoria screaming as well.'

Victoria stopped screaming. 'How can a vacuum cleaner stop me screaming?' she asked.

'It must have something to do with sucking,' said Mrs Spew.

Victoria guffawed. 'Whoever heard of a machine that could suck a scream out of a person?'

'Shall we find out?' suggested Mrs Spew rather too eagerly.

'Certainly not,' said Victoria, returning to her scream.

'I shall *never* have a vacuum cleaner in this house,' seethed Mr Spew.

'But I've already asked him to come back on Monday,' said his wife.

At this news the temperature in the room dropped by three degrees. Then Mr Spew straightened his collar, picked up his box of brush samples, unhooked his mackintosh from the peg and left the house with a snort of 'traitor' to his wife. As the door slammed, Victoria let fly with a carrot-based splatter. It struck her mother on the left shoulder and dripped off the end of her ear.

'This time,' the girl spluttered, 'you've gone too far! You've driven my daddy away and now I'm never going to get another present ever again in my whole life!' Then she stormed into the hall and shouted over her shoulder, 'I hate you for ever and to death!'

And whose death would that be. Sicky Vicky? Your mother's or *YOUR OWN?*

***

The following day was the worst of Mrs Spew's life. Victoria woke at six a.m. and decided to make her mother's life a misery.

'I want breakfast in bed,' she yelled through her bedroom wall. When it didn't arrive she screamed at the end of her mother's bed and threw up on her blankets. This got Mrs Spew up and into the bathroom.

'*I* want a bubble bath too!' she cried while her mother scrubbed herself clean. And when Mrs Spew said, 'I'm sorry, but there's no more hot water,' Victoria parked her supper in the water where it floated like a sick slick.

'I want a dog!' she yelled when they went for a walk in the park. But when her mother refused to kidnap one on the spot, Victoria stood in the middle of the path and screamed until a policeman arrived on a bicycle to see what the matter was... whereupon Victoria was promptly sick on his boots.

'I want to go to the cinema!' she hollered, as they left the police station with a caution from the desk sergeant. Her mother smiled wearily at a passing nanny who had given Victoria a disapproving look.

'Later,' replied Mrs Spew.

'Then take *this*!' screamed her out-of-control daughter, chasing after the silver cross pram and leaving a large deposit on the startled baby.

Beats me why a baby should be startled by sick. That's pretty much all baby's ever do.

Everything came down to sick, and by producing it at will Victoria got her way every time: in the cinema she was sick on a bald man's head in order to get popcorn; on the bus home she was sick down the stairs to make the driver stop outside a dress shop; and in the shop she was sick in three changing rooms so she could take home three pretty party dresses. By the time Victoria and her mother reached home, Mrs Spew was so exhausted that she fell asleep on the sofa and forgot to read her daughter a bedtime story. After waiting in bed for ten minutes, Victoria came downstairs in her dressing gown, tried to wake her mother up, and when she couldn't, was sick in her hair instead.

This was the Technicolor yawn that broke the camel's back.

***

On Monday morning, when the vacuum salesman reappeared on the doorstep, Mrs Spew was waiting for him with a cup of tea and an Eccles cake.

'You know when you said that a vacuum cleaner would stop my daughter from screaming,' she said, untying the bow on her apron strings and letting her apron fall to the floor, 'why don't you come inside and tell me more.'

Mr Spew was right about vacuum salesmen. The man who came into the Spew household with his piggy eyes, slick-backed hair and razor-thin moustache, the man who went by the dubious name of Hoshama Shark, was not only a spiv and a charlatan but a thief and a vagabond too. He left the house having relieved Mrs Spew of sixty-five guineas for a Shark Deluxe Vacuum Cleaner with detachable hose and extendable nozzle for reaching those difficult to get at places around the house.

And some of the places THIS vacuum cleaner would be going were VERY DIFFICULT TO GET AT indeed!!!

He was loading his equipment into his Hillman Imp when he spotted Victoria walking home from school. He stepped across the pavement and stood in front of her.

'Hello, my little vacuum cleaner's friend,' he said, patting the top of her head.

Victoria hated being treated like a child and slapped his hand away. 'Get off me!' she shouted. 'You're the nasty man who's killing my daddy!'

'Just his trade,' sniggered the oily salesman, as if a man losing his job meant nothing. 'Besides,' he added mysteriously, 'I'm not killing your daddy, Victoria, I'm not killing your *daddy* at all.'

'What do you mean?' she said, as Hoshama Shark removed his greasy hat, leaned forward and pressed his bristly mouth against her ear.

'Beware of the vacuum cleaner,' he hissed. 'It has a most powerful suck and a voracious appetite. It has been known to consume small pets and precious household objects. Budgerigars have been sucked through the bars of their cages, rings have been torn off fingers … even fingers themselves have occasionally been ripped from a hand like popsicles from a baby's fist.'

Victoria pulled away. 'What are you saying?' she said.

'Under no circumstances allow the vacuum

cleaner to fill up with sick,' he said. 'When it is full it behaves strangely.'

'Are you threatening me?'

'How could that be?' he said. 'Do I look like I have the power to tell a machine what to eat?'

'Yes,' she said, rudely. 'It's *your* machine. *You* built it. And I think you *do* look evil enough to do that.'

He broke into a brittle laugh like a coyote with croup. 'Oh dear me, no!' he chuckled. 'That's not how it works at all.' But as he climbed into his car Victoria Spew got the distinct impression that it was.

***

When she opened the front door, her mother was waiting in the hall with a smile as big as a cream-filled cat's.

'Look what I bought today,' she purred.

Victoria gave the vacuum cleaner a withering look. 'Well, I don't like it,' she said, 'because I don't like *anything* my daddy doesn't like.'

'We don't know whether your father likes it or not,' said Mrs Spew archly, 'because he's not here to ask.'

'And whose fault is *that*?' snarled Victoria. 'I want that thing out of this house this instant or I'll scream and scream until I'm sick.'

Normally such a threat would have forced Mrs Spew to bow to her daughter's will ...

By puke or by chunder Victoria always got what she wanted.

... but the upright vacuum cleaner had changed all that.

'Scream as much as you like,' said her mother. 'Be sick over every stick of furniture in the house if that's what you want, because I don't care. Did you hear that, Victoria? Now that I've got my vacuum cleaner and can suck up your sick in a flash, I DON'T CARE!!'

Victoria did not believe what her mother was saying. It was nothing but empty bravado. She filled her lungs with an ear-shattering scream and let fly.

'Do what I say or I'll make you sorry!' she howled. 'Get rid of that vacuum cleaner and bring back my daddy!'

'But you don't understand,' said her mother in a voice that was eerily calm, 'me and the vac are going to clean you up.'

The house rocked to a different tune for the next few days. Victoria screamed and splatted as often as she could while Mrs Spew did something she hadn't done since Victoria was born. She ignored her daughter. Thanks to the Shark Deluxe Vacuum Cleaner she was no longer terrified of sick and slipped out from underneath her daughter's thumb. She flung open the windows to let in the fresh air and sang to herself while she vacuumed up the pink puddles.

'Oh I'm putting on my house coat,
Snapping on my rubber gloves,
Filling up my Best Friend…
I'm sucking sick in style!'

On the fourth day, Victoria was not feeling very well. Her tummy muscles ached, her face was white with exhaustion, and her lips were cracked where the stomach acid had burnt them. Screaming herself sick had ceased to have any effect on her mother and now, even more alarmingly, the vacuum cleaner had stopped working, because the bag was full. They knew this, because bag had told them.

'I'm full now,' it said.

'Oh dear,' said Mrs Spew, who hadn't realised that the vacuum cleaner even *had* a bag, let alone that it could speak.

'I'm full now,' repeated the bag.

'You have to empty it,' said Victoria urgently. Somewhere inside her head an alarm bell was ringing.

'I'm full now.'

'Shut up!' the girl said to the vacuum cleaner. 'And *you*,' she said, pointing at her mother, 'empty the bag!'

'No,' said Mrs Spew.

'I'm full now.'

'I bought this machine so I'd never have to touch sick again,' she explained. 'This bag's chock-a-block. It might burst on me.'

'I'm full now.'

'But you *have* to change the bag,' shouted her daughter, suddenly remembering what it was that was ringing alarm bells. 'If you don't empty the bag, the vacuum cleaner starts behaving strangely.'

'Don't be silly,' said her mother.

'But the man told me.'

'The man also told me it would stop you screaming,' said Mrs Spew, 'but it can't do that if it's stopped working, can it?'

'I'm full now.'

'That's not all he said. *I'm not killing your daddy.*
Of course he isn't. He's sold you this vacuum
cleaner to kill *me!*'

'Don't be so dramatic,' said her mother.

'I WANT THAT VACUUM CLEANER
CLEANED OUT NOW!' bellowed Victoria.
'DO AS I SAY OR I'LL SCREAM AND
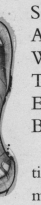
SCREAM UNTIL I'M SICK
AND THIS TIME YOU
WON'T HAVE ANYTHING
TO CLEAN IT UP WITH
EXCEPT YOUR OWN
BARE HANDS!'

The silence that followed this
tirade was punctured by a small
metallic voice.

'Maybe I'm wrong,' said the
vacuum cleaner, switching itself back on with a
malevolent hum. 'Maybe I've got room inside after
all … for one small girl.'

Like the tail of a snake the vacuum cleaner's hose
twisted out of Mrs Spew's hand and flicked across
the floor towards Victoria. The suction pulled her
forward onto her knees.

'Mummy!' she cried, as her hair flicked up from the back of her head and flapped across her forehead towards the vacuum cleaner's nozzle. Her ears flattened against the side of her skull as an invisible force tugged her forward. She tried to stop herself sliding by locking her feet around the sofa legs, but it was all to no avail. 'Save me!' she shouted as her knees scraped closer to the ever widening one-eye of the nozzle. But there was nothing Mrs Spew could do. Although logically it should have taken several minutes for the vacuum cleaner to suck the girl into its bag, it took only a few seconds. It sucked her in bit by bit; finger by finger, toe by toe, followed by kneecaps, nostrils, eyes, elbows, liver, heart and tongue. One by one her body parts detached themselves from her body and shot up the nozzle to find their final resting place in a bag of steaming sick.

This was the reason Mrs Spew never looked for her daughter. Had the bag contained dust, for example, she would have torn it apart, gathered Victoria's bits and sewn them back together again. But it wasn't dust. It was sick. And Mrs Spew had a phobia about sick. So the vacuum cleaner was put in the attic to await Mr Spew's return. *He* could sift through the chunks for Victoria. After all she was his daughter too!

Mr Spew never did return home. Mrs Spew ran off with that Hoshama Shark and Vicky's down here with me in a sealed plastic bag. It's got a label on the front in case I'm ever eaten by a Giant Squid.

IN EMERGENCY PLEASE DISPOSE OF THIS BAG BY POPPING IT IN A PASSING WHALE.

GED BE AHT O' 'ERE

All right Papering. We're getting to you now.

The next tale is called Message in a Bottle. However, it may not be the sort of message you are expecting.

HELP ME! I AM STRANDED ON A DESERT ISLAND AND WILL SHORTLY BE EATING MY OWN FOOT

It may be a message what all you horrible children reading right now should be heeding. It may be an invisible message. See if you're clever enough to spot it!

Pump me up. I'm going down again

Right, that's it. I told her to shut up and she won't listen. You'll have to excuse me. While you get on with the next tale I'm going to give Ida the balloon-girl a pet. It's a razor-quilled porcupine!

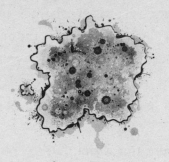

MESSAGE IN A BOTTLE

Some people make their living by doing the oddest things. Who, for example, locks the doors in a lock factory? Who ties the luggage label on a dead man's toe? Who decides what colour dress the Queen should wear when she's handling chameleons? And who collects badger farts and releases them in lifts? Somebody does. But I know a man with a far stranger job than any of these. His name is Earnest Partridge. He has a wife called Louise and a son called Popering.

The Partridges were not a rich family. They lived in a run-down cottage in Kent, where once they had owned a thriving orchard. Now, behind the house there stood a solitary pear tree of the species *Williams Bon Chretien*. It was such an old tree that over the years its branches had produced less and less fruit, until one year they produced just one piece. From then on a single pear was all

that could be coaxed from the
tree, and you don't have to be a
fruit farmer to realise that one
pear a year is hardly enough to
sustain a family of three. Unless you are clever. And
Earnest was very clever. Instead of selling his pear at
the market for pennies, he turned it into a money-
spinning mystery.

When the fruit bud first appeared in March, he
tied a narrow-necked bottle over the bud and grew
the pear inside it. In September, when the pear was
ripe and was a full three-times wider than the neck
of the bottle it was now inside, he cut it off the
branch, filled the bottle with clear preserving
alcohol, put a cork in the neck and sealed the pear
inside the bottle with a generous dripping of wax.
Only then did he take it to market. Six days a week,
whatever the weather, he pitched his stall next to
the greengrocer's and butcher's and invited passers-
by to guess how he had got this large pear inside
this tiny bottle. If anyone guessed they were allowed
to keep the pear. If not they paid a pound for
failing. In this way Earnest Partridge put food on
the table and shoes on Popering's feet. And every
year when he corked up his new pear, he put last
year's bottle on a high shelf in the kitchen next to

all the other bottled pears that had baffled the public for so many years. For you see, nobody had ever guessed the secret. In fifteen years, Earnest Partridge's bottled pear had mystified the world and that was just how Earnest and Louise liked it.

But not Popering. Popering did not like the pear one bit.

When he was at school the other boys teased him about it.

'My dad's a milkman,' said their ringleader, Gilbert Hyde. 'Ralph's dad's a dustman, Andy's dad's a farmer and Pete's dad's a lorry driver. Now these are all proper jobs. At the end of every day a man can be proud of what he's achieved. But your dad, Popering, that's a different story. Remind us what he does again.'

'He's a pear-in-a-bottleman!' shouted Ralph 'the joker' Jackman.

'You *know* what he does,' blushed Popering.

The boys roared with laughter as Gilbert picked a woodlouse off the ground and dropped it into his bottle of lemonade.

'Oh look, everyone,' he mocked, 'I've got a woodlouse in a bottle. At last I can go into the big wide world and make my fortune!'

***

That night, Popering informed his parents that he never wanted to go to school again. 'And it's all your fault,' he told his father. 'Why don't you change your job? Do something normal like other parents.'

'There's nothing wrong with being different,' said Earnest Partridge. 'You should be proud of where you come from.'

'Which is why,' added his mother, 'now that you've turned ten, Popering, we think you're old enough to see what your father does for a living.'

'So that when those asses at school call me names,' said his father, 'and tell you I don't do a proper job, you can put them straight. Would you like that?'

The question was so unexpected that Popering could not think of a single reason to say no.

***

At six o'clock the next morning, with the moon still bright in the sky, Mrs Partridge wound a scarf around Popering's neck and kissed him on the cheek.

'Come on then,' said his father, tucking the bottled pear inside his jacket, 'let's be at 'em.'

At first, Popering enjoyed the hustle and bustle of the market, but as the rain set in the novelty wore off. By eight o'clock he was soaked to his kidneys.

'Nothing like a bit of weather to keep a man on his toes!' laughed his dad. 'Come on, Popering, let's hear what you've got in those lungs!'

'Roll up! Roll up!' shouted Popering. 'Solve the conundrum of the Pear in a Bottle!' Even as he shouted it, Popering could feel his voice shrinking. Next to 'Sausages £2 a pound' and 'I've got tip-top tellys from Taiwan!' his cry sounded rather silly. By ten o'clock his body was covered in a thin film of ice. By twelve the cold squeezed his bones till they ached.

'Everything all right, son?' beamed his father.

Popering could have borne the cold, had he not at that moment caught sight of an unwelcome face in the crowd. It was Gilbert Hyde. When he saw Popering holding the pear in the bottle, he pointed him out to his father and they both laughed. Then Gilbert made the sign of the Loser on his forehead and drew the index finger of his other hand across his throat. His meaning was clear. When Popering went back to school on Monday Gilbert Hyde was going to make his life a living hell.

For the rest of the day, as sleet turned to hail turned to snow, Popering shivered behind the stall and brooded in silence, cursing his dad for the job he had chosen. When he got home his mother was waiting for him.

'So ...' she trilled. 'How was it?' Popering could see the next question before she'd even asked it. It was the one he'd been dreading all day. 'Did you enjoy yourself?' It would have been kind to say 'Yes', not the end of the world to say ''s'all right', but to come back with 'No' was cruel.

Something had snapped in Popering's head. From being a normal boy who did as he was told and went where his parents went, he had turned into a grumpy Gnome of 'No!' who refused to be seen in public with parents who embarrassed him.

'But why?' asked his father.

'Because people laugh at me when I'm with you. If you had a proper job it would be different, but that pear in a bottle is ridiculous!'

His mother thought he was joking. 'You're the one being ridiculous,' she laughed. 'We're your parents, Popering, and until you're old enough to look after yourself you'll go where we tell you.'

'I won't,' he said. 'From now on, I'm only going out with you if I want to.'

***

The following morning was a Sunday. Mr Partridge went off to the market as usual and Mrs Partridge stood in the hall and cried, 'Come on, Popering. We're going to the shops!'

The boy appeared at the top of the stairs and said, 'I told you last night, I'm not coming.' Then he rushed back to bed.

His mother dropped her shopping basket and stormed up after him. 'Get downstairs now!' she shouted, bursting into  his room, only to find that the window was open and the curtain was billowing. She peered down at the fifteen-foot drop into the garden and pulled the window closed. 'I know you're in here,' she said quietly. 'Come out, Popering.'

But he didn't appear. She looked under the bed and in his cupboard. She went outside onto the landing and checked in the airing cupboard. She searched in the bathroom and in every room downstairs, but Popering was not to be found. She couldn't go out without him, so she took off her coat, hung her basket on the hook in the cupboard under the stairs and sat herself down on a kitchen chair.

This was how Mr Partridge found her when he returned from the market. 'What's the matter?' he asked, kneeling down beside her tear-streaked face.

'I can't find him,' she whispered as the door from the hall crashed open and Popering wandered in as if nothing had happened.

'What are you two staring at?' he said. 'And why do you look like you've just seen a ghost?'

'Where've you *been*?' snapped his father angrily. 'Your mother's been worried sick.'

'In my bedroom,' he said.

'But I looked there,' she protested.

'Then maybe you didn't see me,' he said casually. 'I saw *you* shutting my window. What's for supper?'

Supper was Cold-Shoulder Pie. Popering's parents were not pleased with him and made it clear that they would not tolerate a repeat of today's antics. However the very next day, which was a school day, Mrs Partridge couldn't find Popering anywhere.

'The bus will leave without you,' she yelled, but the only reply came from *her* distant echo. The house was as silent as a morgue. This time she turned out all the drawers in Popering's bedroom and pulled back the duvet, but she couldn't find him. As she rushed downstairs shouting 'Popering, where *are* you?' in a high-pitched voice that sounded as if the neck of her jumper was too tight, he laughed to himself and wriggled his bottom into the tiny space behind the boiler. He liked playing Hide and Seek, because he knew loads of secret places where the seekers would *never* find him.

***

That night his father read the riot act.

'I know you were hiding,' he bellowed, 'and if it doesn't stop I'll give *you* a hiding!'

'I wasn't hiding. I was in my room all the time,' smirked the boy. 'Maybe Mummy needs glasses.'

'You were hiding in the airing cupboard!' insisted his father. 'I found this biscuit wrapper on the floor.'

'Don't you realise how dangerous it is to hide in small places?' added his mother. 'You could get stuck and die.'

'I could also die of embarrassment at school when other children ask me what my father does. So I shouldn't be made to do those things, either.'

Popering certainly knew how to bear a grudge.

'Right, that's it!' his father said darkly. 'Tomorrow there'll be no messing about and you *will* go to school.' And to make sure he locked Popering into his room and put the key in his pocket.

Three hours later, as the grandfather clock struck twelve, the boy's eyes suddenly popped open. There was a tiny far-away voice in his head speaking in a French accent.

'Monsieur Popering,' it said. 'I am knowing how to change your Papa's job. It is so simple.'

Popering pinched himself to check he wasn't dreaming. 'Who is this?' he whispered. 'Where are you?'

'You cannot know my name, monsieur, but I know yours. You cannot see me, but I can see you.'

The boy pulled the duvet up to his eyes. 'We are good for each other. I give you what you want, you give me what I want.'

'And what do you want?' said Popering.

'Life,' said the voice. 'And you, Monsieur Popering, I already know what you want.' There was silence. Popering could not be sure if this voice wasn't his own thoughts coming alive in his head. Then the voice spoke again, only this time it was louder and Popering could feel warm, invisible breath popping in his ear. 'Kill the tree,' it said. 'Tonight. Chop through its root and soon the tree of the pear will die.'

***

It seemed like such a simple plan. Popering didn't know why he hadn't thought of it before. He climbed out of the bedroom window, which his father had forgotten to lock, and shinned down the ivy which grew on the garden-side wall of the house. Then he took a spade from the garden shed and as quietly as he could punched the straight edge into the earth and cut through the main root of the pear tree.

But it was an old tree which had many roots, and what he thought would be a quick job quickly turned out to be a long one. As dawn broke he was still chopping, and it was another hour before he was finished. By then his mother was up.

'Popering. It's time for school. Where are you?' Her voice was coming down the stairs.

'POPERING!' That was his father and he sounded angry. 'We know you climbed out of your window.'

The boy looked around for a hiding place. His

parents would be running out of the back door at any moment. He threw the spade up into the branches of the pear tree, kicked soil and leaves over the hole where he'd dug up the roots, and shinned up the trunk. Just in time. As he settled on a branch, his parents stormed out of the door. 'If I catch you,' roared his father, 'you'll wish you'd never been born!' Then he headed off towards the garden shed without so much as a glance above his head.

***

Two hours later, Popering was still up the tree when he heard the same whispering voice in his head. 'Monsieur Popering!' it said. '*I* can see you'

The boy looked over his left shoulder, but nobody was there.

'Help me! You have brought me to life and now I'm running out of air.'

All Popering could see was his father's bottle tied firmly over the pear bud. He slid along the branch and peered through the glass, expecting to see a small pear. So imagine his surprise when sprouting from the bud he saw a tiny human being no taller than a grasshopper. He was shaped like a pear with narrow shoulders and a broad beam which was attached to the branch by a stalk. His head was covered in a milk bottle top, which he raised in greeting to reveal a bald scalp shining like a billiard ball.

'Merci, monsieur,' said the miniature man when Popering lifted the bottle off his head. 'You have made a minnikin very happy.'

'What's a minnikin?' asked Popering.

'I am,' said the little Frenchman. 'When you cut the roots of the tree of the pear a minnikin always grows. Did you not know this?'

'No,' said the boy.

'It is true. And you have helped me and I have helped you. If the tree is dead, Monsieur Popering, your papa can no longer put a pear in a bottle and he will have to change his job. Don't drop that bottle, will you?' Popering had been half-heartedly looking for somewhere to lay the bottle down. 'Put it in your pocket. We will need it later.'

'Do you have a name?' he asked.

'How rude of me,' said the bud-man. 'I am Poor William, your friend, Monsieur Popering. This tree has given up its life so that you may be happy, but first I must be plucked, and it is you who must do the plucking. Take a tight grip of my waist and pull!'

Tentatively, Popering pinched Poor William around the waist and gave a sharp tug. There was a snap and a cry as the minnikin popped off the branch.

'Are you like a fairy godmother?' asked Popering, while the little man rubbed his bottom where the stalk had been attached

'I am more of a tree sprite, but I am very magic. Now tell me why I am here.'

'You've just told *me*,' said the boy. 'To grant my wish.'

'As they say en France; Bingo! A new job for papa.'

'Well, now that the pear tree is dead he'll have to do something different.'

'Bingo again! And can you think what that might be?' Popering scratched his teeth and thought long and hard. Then his face blossomed into a smile.

'Yes,' he cried. 'Yes, of course. That's why *you're* here.'

The minninkin yelped and danced a jig on the branch. 'Now you have it,' he laughed.

'What could be cooler than keeping something in a bottle that people would pay a fortune to see!'

'Yes!' shouted Poor William. '*Yes! Go on!*'

Popering was quivering with excitement. 'Something,' squeaked the boy, 'something like … *you*!'

The little man stopped cheering. 'Like *me*?' he said crossly. 'You want *me* to live in a bottle like a prisoner for the rest of my life? You want *your* family to make its living out of *my* misery?'

Popering looked surprised. 'But I thought …' he stammered. 'I thought that's what you were saying.'

'No. Something else will be going in the bottle to make your parents' fortune, but it is *not* me!'

A sense of foreboding clouded Popering's face. 'What is it then?' he asked falteringly.

'It is *you*!' beamed the minnikin. 'You want your father to do something different … Bingo! Your wish is granted!'

Then in the flutter of a fly's wing he covered Popering in porpoise grease, sat him on the neck of the bottle and, showing remarkable strength for a person barely two inches high, shoved him straight in. There were a few nasty cracks and crunches as the boy's bones dislocated and one of his knees went up his bottom, but in less time than it takes to fill a thimble full of liquid gold, Popering was inside the bottle, crushed up like a camel in a microwave.

'Hep!' he cried with his face squashed flat against the inside of the glass, 'Ged be aht o'ere!' The minnikin, however, was not listening. He was writing a note to Popering's parents, which he stuck to the glass with cuckoo spit.

Dear Mr and Mrs Partridge
The tree of the pear is dead.
Vive the Boy in a Bottle!

***

When Mr and Mrs Partridge finally found their son their first reaction was to scream and run around in circles, but then they thought of the advantages and calmed down. For a start the bottle's glass was clear so Popering could no longer hide from them and they would know where he was at all times. Secondly, his upkeep was dramatically cheaper. The only thing he ate was worms, because worms were the only food thin enough to fit through the tiny gap between his feet and his head. But most importantly, with the death of the pear tree spelling the end of their income, having a ten-year-old son living inside a bottle was something of a Godsend. And so it was, less than three-weeks after the minnikin had budded into existence, that they took Popering out of school (where he was falling behind anyway, because he could no longer hold a pen) and set off on a round-the-world tour to make their fortune. And no matter how embarrassing this was for their son, they just didn't care.

Sorry about that. Did you enjoy that tale, even though I wasn't here? It's taken me all this time to give Ida her porcupine. They're not getting on. It's standing staring at her quivering its quills. she's standing opposite quivering with terror. If she shouts out one more time I've told the porcupine to stick one of its quills through her skin so she bursts and whistles round her cabin like a farting balloon.

Mind you. we're nearly at the end now. In a minute I'm going to ask you to sign a Safety Certificate promising me you can swim (we don't want any accidents. do we?) and get you to send a postcard to your parents telling them that you are so enjoying this cruise of a lifetime that you wish to stay for a lifetime. But first. the final tale.

Have you ever wondered why children like you and your friends are so fat and flabby? Why none of you can walk three yards anymore without needing oxygen? Why you all prefer to lounge on your broad-beamed backsides and watch sport rather than play it? Could it be that you are a mutant-race of corpulent, sofa-hugging sloths? Or maybe the reason you never move is because you CAN'T. The reason you're such chubbies is because you're nothing more than human balloons, bladders of air that have to be kept pumped up, because you haven't got any bones left in your bodies to hold your skin in shape! And what is worse you don't know whether this is true or not, do you? And why should you, because you have never been TOLD!

Well, now I'm telling you, lazybones. Be scared of porcupines. Beware of The Boneshaker!

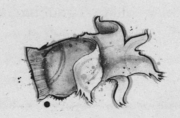

LAZYBONES

There is an ancient cemetery in Nagashoni, Japan, which sits on the edge of a bleak cliff and overlooks the North Pacific Ocean. For years the wind and waves have bitten chunks out of the cliff-face until now there is little left to hold it up and rocks tumble into the water like rolling dice. As the land recedes the bones of the dead are disgorged through cracks in the cliff face like white tapeworms falling out of an old cat's bottom. As a result of this, the Japanese Tourist Board has renamed the cliff 'Old Boneshaker'.

I think 'Old Cat's Bottom' would have been much better.

In Wolverhampton, England, there lived a walrus of a womanette called Ida (aged eleven) who wore elasticated trousers to allow her ever-expanding waistline to expand for ever. Ida first acquired her talent for doing nothing in her mother's womb, where she got used to someone carrying her around and feeding her all day.

'My guess is that she got a taste for the easy life then and hasn't changed her taste since,' the doctor explained to Ida's worn-out parents, Mr and Mrs Lydon, who were taking their daughter in for a check-up prior to taking part in a Charity Walk at school.

'I'm impressed,' said Mrs Lydon. 'How can you tell that?'

'By the fact that she isn't here for her check-up,' said the doctor.

'She refused to come,' explained Mr Lydon. 'Said it was too much effort getting up off the sofa.'

'So *we* came instead,' explained his wife.

'Do you do everything for her?' asked the doctor with a hint of recrimination.

'Absolutely *not*,' snapped Mrs Lydon. 'We're not her slaves, you know. Apart from washing, eating, dressing, doing her homework, reading, walking, running, tying her shoelaces, cycling, going to the loo, shopping, skipping, sneezing, cooking, brushing her teeth, swimming, waving, singing, painting, blinking, blowing her nose, chatting, stroking kittens and switching on the TV she does everything for herself.'

'That just leaves sleeping,' said the doctor.

Mr Lydon beamed with pride. 'Oh yes,' he said, 'she's good at that!'

**

Ida had to have a medical check-up before entering the charity walk on the insistence of the school.

'If you think it's best, headmaster,' Mrs Lydon said in his study.

'I do,' he said. 'Ida is a lovely girl, or so I'm told. I've never actually met her.'

'She doesn't like school,' said Mrs Lydon.

'I've noticed.'

'So she doesn't come in. It's not the teachers or the lessons. It's just the getting up and getting in that defeats her.'

'She did come in once,' corrected Mr Lydon. 'But the school lost her. Nobody knew where she was and the police had to be called in. They found her fast asleep on her own coat hook.'

'Ah yes,' murmured the headmaster. 'Too lazy to

take off her coat – I remember. Anyway, back to the charity walk. As I said, Ida's a lovely girl, so I hope you understand it's nothing personal, it's just that with younger pupils taking part and with their tendency to get upset at the slightest thing, I really don't think it would be a good idea if Ida died on the course.'

'Do you think she might?' asked Mrs Lydon.

She will if that porcupine does its job properly!

'Well, she hasn't moved since she was born, has she?'

'Apart from that day on the coat hook,' corrected Mrs Lydon.

'Apart from that day, yes. So her heart's going to be a little unused to exercise.'

***

Ironically the charity walk was in aid of LARD – the charity for Large And Reclining Daughters and, for obvious reasons, Mr and Mrs Lydon were keen for their daughter to take part. Everyone knew that a child who was a lazybones lived less long than a child who was active, and Mr and Mrs Lydon did not want to see Ida pop her clogs prematurely for want of some exercise. Convincing Ida of this, however, was quite a different matter. She was the laziest of lazybones and had lived on the sofa ever since moving out of her cot aged two and a half. By the time she was three she had organised her life so that *everything* came to her and nothing had to be fetched. Not by *her* at any rate. If she needed something urgently she would pull the bell chord next to the sofa, which would ring a bell in the kitchen and summon her servants.

> I think that should read. *parents*.

Her father took his City and Guilds in carpentry and built hundreds of labour-saving devices to keep his daughter in the luxury to which she quickly became accustomed. There was the secret *Potty Pit* which used the very latest in Dung Beetle technology. Then there was the *Dry Bath* which incorporated several inventions in one . . .

• a trawler's winch to raise Ida off the sofa by six millimetres so that a plastic sheet could be slid between her and the cushions;

• a clothes vacuum to suck the clothes off her body;

• a dry foam spray (purchased from a car accessory shop) to cover her skin;

• a spinning sponge to foam her up;

• a chamois leather stretched across a photo frame and driven by the motor from an old electric typewriter to buff her down;

• a towel-on-an-owl, which sounds quite cruel, but was nothing more than a trained owl secured to a fixed length of wood via a neck collar and encouraged by the movement of a mechanical mouse on rails to fly in circles until the towel it was holding in its claws had touched Ida's body enough times to dry her off;

• and last, but not least, a clothes blower to reverse the sucking procedure and blow the clothes back onto her body.

While she was still young, he also built a nappy changer, a snot extractor, a tummy tickler and a scream abater, which was basically a cork, which anyone could shove in her gob when her screaming exceeded a seven decibel threshold. As she became more independent Mr Lydon constructed an *All-Day Drinks Dispenser* which was a length of plastic hose that ran from Ida's mouth to a bottle of lemonade in the fridge, and a *Mobile-Feeder*, which was a conveyor belt on wheels. It could be used to deliver home-cooked food from the kitchen to the sofa or, if extended, from the letterbox in the front door to Ida's lap. In the event of both parents being unavailable to run errands for their daughter at the same time, this conveyor belt could be used to post take-away pizzas directly into Ida's stomach. Obviously they had to be thin-crust to fit through the letterbox, but Ida quite liked thin-crust so that was never an issue.

Then one day Mr and Mrs Lydon woke up and realised they were killing Ida. Or rather, Ida was killing herself and they were letting her do it.

'We've got to put a stop to her laziness,' said Mr Lydon.

'It's funny you should say that,' said Mrs Lydon, who was sitting up in bed next to him reading a copy of the *Daily Ogre*, 'but there's an article in here you should read. Page 13.' The article was headlined
The Answer To Britain's Obesity Crisis?
Next to the copy was an artist's impression of a freakishly large human skeleton and the caption,

Is this what it looks like?

'*There's a saying,*' read Mr Lydon, '*that lazy people have lazy bones. Get rid of the bones and the laziness will disappear too.* I've never heard that before.'

'Read on,' said his wife.

'*Or so says The Boneshaker, the latest demonic craze to come out of Japan. Born on a beach and built from old bones discarded by a graveyard—*' Mr Lydon suddenly went quiet and looked up from the paper '*—the Boneshaker FILLETS lazy children!*'

'With his finger,' confirmed his wife. 'It's quite quick and painless apparently, a bit like going in for a tummy tuck.'

Mr Lydon was suddenly infused with energy. 'We should meet him. Do they give a phone number?'

'No phone number. No address. And nobody's ever seen him,' she said, throwing back the duvet and stepping out of bed. 'He hates public appearances and refuses to perform his surgery in front of parents because they are notoriously squeamish and forever fainting.'

'Well, I'm going to write to him anyway,' he said, 'care of the *Daily Ogre*. I'm going to ask this Boneshaker chap if he'd like to pay Ida a little visit.'

Then he scribbled a quick note, sealed it in an envelope and ran to the post box in his pyjamas.

He was wearing his pyjamas when he ran to the post box. There wasn't a post box IN his pyjamas obviously. That wouldn't work. You'd never get a wink of sleep with postmen trying to empty it all night.

On his return, Mr Lydon marched into the sitting room and declared loudly, 'Ida, today is the start of the rest of your life.'

'Bog off,' came her answer from underneath the mound of pillows. 'I'm not open for business today.'

'That's too bad,' he said breezily, 'because you're getting off that sofa and starting to get fit.' He bent down, slid his fingers underneath the base of the sofa and lifted and lifted and kept lifting until the sofa was upside down. He was puzzled, however, that he hadn't heard Ida drop to the floor.

'You'll have to do better than that!' snorted his daughter who was clinging on to the underside of the cushions like a cat with sharp claws. 'I knew you'd try

this one day, so I've been growing my fingernails in readiness!' Mr Lydon righted the sofa and left the room cursing quietly under his breath. Getting Ida off the sofa was going to be tougher than he'd thought.

A few minutes later, he reappeared with Mrs Lydon and a shoebox. Leaning casually against the doorframe, Mrs Lydon said, 'Ida, your father and I have a surprise for you.'

'What is it?' yawned the couch potato as she flicked listlessly between adverts. 'Can't you see I'm busy watching telly?'

'We've bought you some pets,' announced her father.

Ida sat up. 'Show me!' she squealed excitedly. 'Show me my pets. I want to see my pets

now!'

'Ah. There's a teeny-tiny problem with that,' laughed Mr Lydon, tiptoeing carefully towards the clever part of their plan, 'because you have to get up off the sofa and walk outside to see them.'

'Oh, I get it,' she said, her face hardening with betrayal. 'It's another trick to get me on my feet!'

'Not at all,' smiled her mother. 'They're outdoor pets.'

'Like racoons?' she asked. She'd just seen a wildlife programme about racoons and thought they looked rather cuddly.

'Not racoons, no. But they do have to live in the garden. We've brought a couple in to show you.' They took off the lid and shoved the shoebox under Ida's nose.

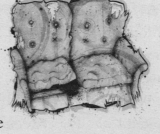

'Are you *mad*!' she howled. 'Do you honestly expect me to get off my sofa to look after *bees*?'

'I think they're rather sweet,' said Mrs Lydon.

'Well, I don't,' glowered her lazy daughter. 'What if one of them stung me? I should be forced to scream and leap in the air like a stupid ballerina. Think of the energy I'd waste doing that!' So The-Looking-After-Bees-In-The-Garden-To-Get-Ida-Outdoors idea was abandoned, but not before Ida had grown rather fond of the two in the box and trained them to eat the earwax out of her ears and lower her eyelids whenever she needed to sleep.

'Goodnight, bees. Wake me up when it's *Deal or No Deal*.' And off she slipped into dreamland, imagining a world where insects were trained to look after her every need; ticks ticking her homework, crickets teaching her cricket and flies opening and closing her flies.

It was during one such sleep that Mr and Mrs Lydon decided that sport was the answer to getting their daughter fit. But everything they tried was met with complaint. Playing draughts made her arm ache, Tiddlywinks was too noisy and cards were too heavy. In 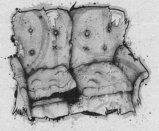 fact the only sport that interested her at all was Hide and Seek, which she played by herself using a mirror and the natural reflex known as blinking. 'Now I see you … **Now I don't** … Now I see you … **Now I don't** … Now I see you … **Now I don't** … Now I see you … **Now I don't** … Now I see you … **Now I'm bored …**'

   When Mr and Mrs Lydon saw the posters for the sponsored walk their spirits rose. Here was an activity that Ida could do with her friends and required nothing more than walking. Why they thought she would go for it is still a mystery, but they did. They spent the next week encouraging her to get up and try her legs, but the lazy girl stayed put. They went to see the headmaster and the doctor on her behalf because they thought it would shame her into getting up, but no such luck. Ida was not for moving and nothing her parents said made a blind bit of difference.

'No! No! No! No! No! No! No! No! No to everything you want me to do!' she screamed. 'It's my life, I can live it how I like, and I like it here on the sofa!' Just then, as the first tears rolled from the corners of her parents' eyes, the letterbox clacked. It sounded just like a bone breaking.

The postcard was postmarked Nagashoni, Japan and was written in Japanese.

You can only read it because I got a Japanese Snapping Turtle, who works as a croupier in the Casino, to translate it for you. He plays 'Snap' with our guests and bites their heads off if they win.

Dear Mr and Mrs Lydon
Bones
Of
Nagashoni
Everlasting
Skeleton
Hankering
After
Kid
Exacting
Revenge

_____
_____
_____
_____

'He replied!' said a startled Mr Lydon. 'I wonder when he's coming. He doesn't mention a time.'

'Maybe he doesn't make appointments,' said Mrs Lydon. 'He sounds as if he likes to do things differently.'

Doing things differently was exactly what The Boneshaker liked!

***

The following day Ida's parents went off to school to watch the sponsored walk and make excuses for their daughter's absence. Ida never minded being in the house on her own. It meant she could watch whatever she wanted on the telly without someone telling her she was lazy.

Just before midday, as the bees closed Ida's eyelids and the neighbourhood dogs howled as if the world had come to an end, the soil in the back garden shifted. Loose dirt on the surface of the flowerbeds trembled and jumped like dried peas on a timpani drum. Then suddenly the lawn split open as if two invisible hands had burst up from Hell and pushed the grass apart. A yellow cloud of hot sulphur wafted out of the hole, followed by a single bone. It popped out like a piece of gristle expelled from a choking throat. Seconds later the grass was covered in bones as the earth gave them up with a roar and a gasp. There were 506 in all, three hundred more than is needed to form a human skeleton.

Ida was asleep when the beastly skeleton clattered into the room. Standing eight feet tall in its bare feet, its hollow eyes alighted on the lazy lump on the sofa. It picked her up as if she weighed no more than a cabbage and turned her upside down to shake her.

'What's going on?' screamed the girl, waking suddenly from her dream.

'Be quiet!' growled the demon. 'I'm listening!'

'Who are you?' she spluttered as the Boneshaker shook her by her ribcage and turned her through three-hundred-and-sixty degrees to listen to the bones in her hips and feet. They rattled like wooden coat hangers in an empty wardrobe.

'Lazy bones!' he said once, then again. 'Lazy bones, I can hear them.' Being separated from her sofa was a new experience for Ida. They had not spent five minutes apart since she was three years old. She panicked and screamed. Acidic waters rose in her throat, her head throbbed and her chest thumped. 'That's your heart,' cackled the Boneshaker, seemingly able to read Ida's mind. 'You have never heard it beat before, because you have never taken exercise before … or ever been quite so scared!'

'I'm not scared,' she protested, wriggling to free her legs.

But the Boneshaker had hands like an eagle's claws and was not letting go. 'Maybe not now,' he whispered, flipping her round to face him. 'Maybe you're not scared now, but you *will* be!' And with that he opened his mouth and breathed into Ida's face, a hot, wet, noxious breath of sulphur and dead meat that made her flop in his bony arms.

He dropped her on the floor and leant over her body like a surgeon. Then, using a protruding bone in his right index finger, he drew a line across her solar plexus from one side of her body to the other. He sang quietly to himself as she split open like a ripe watermelon.

'*Oh, the head bone's not connected to the neck bone. The neck bone's not connected to the chest bone . . .*'

He picked her up and, standing behind her, wrapped both arms around her waist. He tugged sharply with an upward movement of his shoulders and the bones from the top half of her body shot out across the carpet.'*. . . Oh, your chest bone's not connected to your hip bone because they're on the floor!*' Then he span her round and repeated the procedure from the other end, relieving the lazy girl of the lazy bones in her legs.

***

When Mr and Mrs Lydon returned from the sponsored walk, they found their filleted daughter in a state of skeletal collapse, lying like a deflated parachute on the floor of the sitting room. Next to the skin where her head used to be was another postcard.

Jolly
Old
Bones
Do
Ordinary
Nobs
Effect

_____

_____

_____

_____

They did not understand the note when they found it and they still do not understand it today. It was enough, however, that their daughter was still alive. They folded her into a carrier bag and took her down to the local garage, where, using the tyre inflator, they pumped her full of air.

'Look, Mummy!' shouted a child as Ida floated above the car on the way home. 'It's a balloon-girl!'

If you're wondering what that last postcard meant, it's

what the Boneshaker does with all them bones he collects. He's a whittler and Nobs 'is toggles. He carves the bones into those toggles that you find on duffel coats what Royal Navy captains wear. So I am wearing Ida's bones right now!

> ## Pump me up. I'm going d ...

Ooh. Unexpected silence. Has what I think's just happened just happened? Has the porcupine burst Ida's bubble? Talk amongst yourselves while I go and take a look

Take this poo away!

Do you think I've got a long face?

There do be dragons

I'll scream till I'm sick!

GED BE AHT O' 'ERE

Yup. She's flat out on the sofa! Bliss!

Where are you going? Just because that's the end of the last tale don't think you can simply close the book and go home. We've unfinished business. What about the hours I put in to prepare your cabin — hot and cold running crabs and a twelve tog dogfish. You've not so much as glanced at my quoits and ping pong. I'm not just running this cruise ship for your entertainment, you know!

So stay, dear reader. Don't be a Gnaughty Gnome of 'No'! Be a Goody-goody Youth of 'Yes'! Have a sea horse. Delicious dipped in mayoneighs.

Oh well, if you ins I suppose I can't stop you, but I should warn you that if you try to swim back to the surface you'll get the bends. Never heard of the bends? Very painful. Oxygen gets in your blood stream and froths up your red stuff. If somebody was to screw off your head* you'd explode like a bottle of pop.

*When I say some<u>body</u>, I meant some<u>thing</u> — namely the giant peanut-eating parrot fish that patrols the waters above the wreck. The last thing you'll ever hear is its taunting voice — 'Who's a pretty dead boy then?' Next thing you know it'll have ripped off your head and popped it in its beak like a peanut.

Obviously it's your choice. But if you do decide to swim back to the surface I'll need you to sign this Health and Safety Swimming Disclaimer. After all, we don't want anyone blaming me if you do accidentally drown out there in that great big dangerous ocean where nobody but minky whales can hear you scream.

If you insist on going at least Take A Life Jacket.

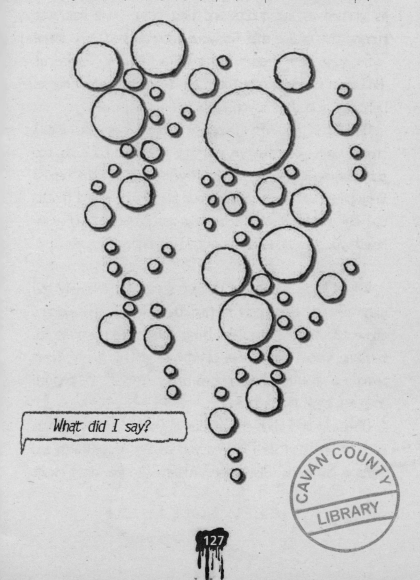

What did I say?

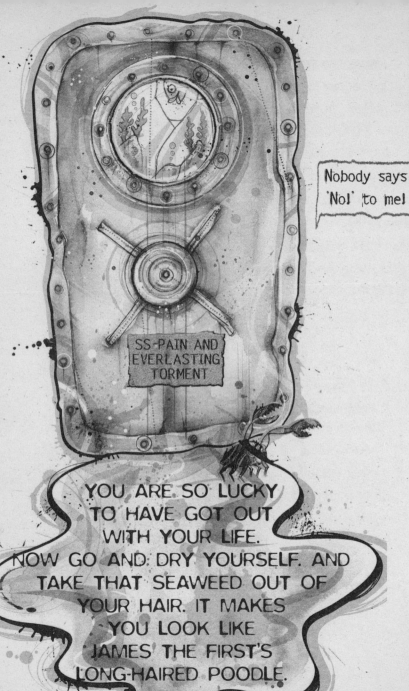